A LADY

OF

KING ARTHUR'S COURT

SARA HAWKS STERLING

Illustrated by Clara Elsene Peck

NEW YORK

MEGARA PUBLISHING

MEGARA
PUBLISHING

Megara Publishing Inc.
447 Broadway
New York, NY 10013
megarapublishing.com

This is a work of fiction. Names, characters, organizations, places, events, and incidents are either products of the author's imagination or are used fictitiously. Any resemblance to actual persons, living or dead, or actual events is purely coincidental.

A Lady of King Arthur's Court is available in the public domain. The work was originally published in 1907 by George W. Jacobs & Co. The edits and formatting of this work are exclusive to Megara Publishing.

Title: A Lady of King Arthur's Court
Author: Sara Hawks Sterling
Illustrator: Clara Elsene Peck
ISBN: 978-1-7373477-0-5

All Rights Reserved.

No part of this book may be reproduced in any form or by any means, electronic, mechanical, photocopying, recording, or otherwise, without express written permission of the publisher.

Megara Publishing and the Megara logo are trademarks of Megara Publishing Inc., or its affiliates.

Manufactured in the United States of America

TABLE OF CONTENTS

ILLUSTRATIONS

A LADY OF KING ARTHUR'S COURT
BEING A ROMANCE OF THE HOLY GRAIL

SARA HAWKS STERLING
Illustrated by Clara Elsene Peck

ABOUT THIS EDITION

The text and illustrations of this edition are from the original 1907 edition by George W. Jacobs & Company. Certain punctuations, contractions and abbreviations have been modified from the original 1907 text to reflect modern grammatical rules.

No modifications have been made to this work that would in any way change the meaning or intent of it by the author. Any alternate spellings contained in this work are as the author intended.

This work contains negative depictions and mistreatment towards individuals with dwarfism. These depictions were wrong then, and are wrong now. They have not been altered from their original form, in the hopes that readers will be able to acknowledge the problematic nature of such tropes in both historical and current fantasy, and work to create a more inclusive future for the genre.

I am Ulfius of Ireland ..

CHAPTER ONE

Arthur's Court at Pentecost

It befell on a time, at the Feast of Pentecost, that Arthur, king of England, according to his custom on that holy day, would not sit at meat until he had witnessed some marvel. By late afternoon he was waiting still. Then Sir Kaye came to him and said:

"Sir, here are strange adventures coming. I espied but now, as I looked out over the country, a dwarf, richly clad, riding on horseback; and attending him a tall young man, seeming of noble blood by his bearing, but in poor attire. So to your meat, sire, for surely, methinks, there be some matter toward."

So the king went to meat, and with him many other kings, and noble knights, and fair ladies. And afterwards, there came into the hall the two men, even as Sir Kaye had described them.

"God you bless, and all your fair fellowship," cried the dwarf, bowing low before the dais whereon sat the king and his queen, Guenever. "I am come hither to pray you to give me three gifts, King Arthur."

"Ask, and ye shall have your asking," the king answered, "if I may worshipfully and honorably grant them to you."

"That may you do, my lord king," said the dwarf. "One I shall ask forthwith, and the other two a twelve-month hence. I crave now that ye will grant me the first adventure that cometh to court."

At these bold words there was a shout of laughter throughout the Court and the Table Round. The dwarf scarce reached to the king's elbow, and he was passing uncomely. In that great company of goodly knights and fair ladies, his apparent lack of strength and beauty was the more marked.

Three only did not laugh beside the dwarf himself. One was the king, who, having seen many men and many marvels, was accustomed to the unexpected. Another was the dwarf's attendant, the tall young man in mean raiment, who stood a little behind his master, his face muffled in his hood. The third was the Lady Dieudonnée de Cameliard, one of Guenever's waiting-women. Standing in her place near the queen, she fixed her eyes half fearfully upon the dwarf's servant the instant he entered the hall, and kept them there as if striving to draw his gaze toward hers. But if so she wished she did not succeed; for the youth's eyes were lowered discreetly, and looked at none.

Arthur raised his hand to command silence.

"My son," he said gravely to the dwarf, "'tis a strange boon that thou cravest, and meseems there is some mystery here that I cannot fathom. Bethink thee, thou art not as other men; and those of thy kind are more apt to serve than to be served. Thy man there— he is of goodly seeming. 'Tis pity he is not of gentle blood. Come hither, prythee, youth."

The servant moved forward obediently, and stood beside the dwarf. Thus side by side, the contrast between the two was yet more apparent. Queen Guenever gazed admiringly at the youth's broad shoulders and long limbs, and thought that never had she seen a goodlier man—save one.

The king began a question to the servant, but the dwarf's harsh voice interrupted.

"He hears, please you, King Arthur, but cannot speak. He is dumb, having been rescued by me from the Saracens, who among other tortures cut out his tongue."

"Alas, poor youth!" sighed Queen Guenever, and a pretty murmuring echo ran along all the line of ladies. But Dieudonnée de Cameliard lowered her eyes, and a smile touched her lips.

"'Tis pity," said the king regretfully. "Well, to thy boon. Sir—what art thou hight?"

"I am Ulfius of Ireland," the dwarf replied, "and I crave only the boon of service. Knight I am not yet."

"Well, take thy boon, Ulfius," said the king. "Jesu be praised, we have many brave knights at court; but God forbid that I should refuse the service of any true man, no matter what his outward seeming. Thou art of Ireland, thou sayest. Were Anguish, thy king's son, here, he might know thee; but yester-morn he asked permission to seek what might befall him, so he is gone from us. Stand thou ready, Ulfius. The first adventure that comes to court shall be thine; and if it is achieved, the other boons thou cravest shall be thine also if they lie with my honor. Here comes Sir Kaye, with news by his countenance. What cheer, pray. Sir Kaye?"

"So please you," Sir Kaye replied, "a damosel has come hither, riding on a palfrey, to crave succor from you and the Table Round."

Scarcely had he spoken the words when the great doors of the hall clanged together behind the damosel, who stood an instant hesitating, with the eyes of the court upon her.

She was robed in black, lustreless and dead, that clung around her slender figure in long, yielding lines. Her hair was black, and her eyes deep wells of darkness. Upon her arm she bore a golden shield, blank of device or motto. When Sir Kaye, at the king's command, went down to meet her and usher her to the throne, all eyes were fastened upon her, all ears strained to hear the outcome of this adventure.

"Whence come you, and what would you, fair damosel?" asked Arthur, when she had knelt before him.

"Sire, I have traveled far," she answered, "and I come to crave succor for a fair lady, who lies hard bested in her castle by a giant, and calls through me for aid of your mercy from a knight of the Table Round."

"Jesu forbid," the king answered, "that I should deny your prayer; for never may it be said that fair damosel came for succor to Arthur's court, and received it not. What say you, my lords? Which of you shall ride with the damosel on this adventure?"

A dozen knights sprang forward; but ere any reached the king, Ulfius rushed nimbly to the throne.

"Sir," he cried, "I beseech you, remember the boon you granted to me e'en now."

CHAPTER TWO

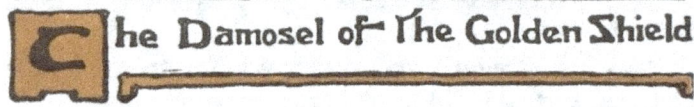

The Damosel of The Golden Shield

Queen Guenever gave an exclamation of annoyed repugnance, echoed by more than one of the court; but King Arthur looked down gravely at the dwarf.

"It is so," he said. "Damosel, to this man hath it been granted to follow the first adventure that comes to court. Wherefore he and no other may undertake this of thine."

Into the maiden's eyes, as she looked at the dwarf, came an expression of wonder that was almost horror.

"My lord and king, this is no trifling adventure. I beseech you mercy. My lady's need is great; for she is hard beset, and many of her loyal followers have perished. Prythee send a more fitting champion to my mistress."

"This lies not now in my power, gentle damosel," he replied; "but cheer thee. Great wonders have been achieved in the world by seeming trifling means. Perchance, too, Ulfius will admit a companion adventurer in this quest."

Before the suppliant could speak, Ulfius destroyed the hope.

"All my strength and power I offer to thy noble mistress," he said; "but none other may ride away from this court with us and none may follow until I be the victor or the vanquished."

"The victor—" said the damosel contemptuously. With a quick movement, she rested the shield on the floor beside the dwarf. The top of it was on a level with the chin of Ulfius.

"Behold the champion you have given me," she cried. "Lord king, my mistress sent this shield as reward to the knight who should rescue her. It is as yet unemblazoned with coat-of-arms or motto; but one day it will bear upon it those of the hero who succors my lady. See! E'en should this runtling win the quest, here is no shield for him."

Ulfius looked up at her unmoved and uncaring.

"You say well, fair maiden," he remarked. "But courage lieth not always in bulk. It may hap that I shall win thy lady and her shield; and if it should so chance, it shall be carried for me by my dumb armorbearer." He beckoned his servant, who had slipped back into the shadows. "Come hither, boy, and lift this shield for me."

When the damosel saw the youth who came forward and lifted the golden shield, the blood which the sight of the chosen champion had driven from her face again glowed in her cheeks.

"A pity the man were not the master," she said; but her voice had softened, and was no longer sharply desperate. "Good king, I prayed to the Ruler of the world, in sunlight and in starlight, as I hastened hither, that some knight of mighty prowess might undertake this adventure—"

Her voice broke. She let fall her outstretched hands and her head sank upon her breast. A murmur of pity filled the great hall at the evident anguish of her disappointment.

"It is thy fortune, damosel, that this so chances," the king answered. "Otherwise it may not be. I do not lightly break troth. But this I promise—if promise may lighten thy heavy distress—that if this champion be not victor, and thou wilt return to court with such tidings, I myself will ride with thee thence."

The damosel knelt and kissed the hem of his robe. Her thanks were in too low a voice for the knights to hear. When she rose, she lifted not her eyes to the king's face.

"God speed you, Ulfius," said Arthur quietly. "A twelvemonth hence, come hither and recount your adventures."

It was a strange group that went down the great hallway; the slender maiden towering high above the sturdy dwarf, and following them, the mute servitor, bearing the shield. As they neared the threshold, a jingle of bells was heard, the doors were flung wide unceremoniously, and there stood before them Dagonet, the court fool. Accompanying him was another figure, stately, hooded, and attired in changing shades of blue.

"Here is a coil, my Uncle Merlin," cried Dagonet, grimacing. He was tall and abnormally thin, fond of twisting his long body into curious contortions. Now he bent over double, and thrust his head forward into the damosel's sulky face.

"What ails thee, sweeting? Doth the knight Uncle Arthur gave thee like thee not? Wilt take me instead?"

"As lief thee as a dwarf and a mute," replied the maiden, flinging herself away from him. In the movement, she jostled accidentally against the broad-shouldered, hooded figure accompanying the fool. She started and looked up; then shrank back shuddering.

"Ah, teach me thy power, Uncle Merlin," cried the jester. "What is it in thy eyes—"

"Peace," said Merlin sternly. His voice was low, his speech deliberate. "Peace, Dagonet. There is more here than thou knowest."

"And dost thou know. Uncle Merlin?" inquired the fool affectionately, winding his long arms around his companion's neck. "I'll tell thee now. I think we are both fools alike; only other men have found me out; and thee they have not yet discovered."

Merlin calmly removed the other's twining arms.

"I know thee who thou art," he said in a low voice to the maiden. "Pass on. All shall be well."

Her face ashen with fear, she crept past him. Ulfius looked up confidently.

"Hast no word of cheer for me?" he asked, in a tone as familiar as Dagonet's.

"Ay," replied Merlin quietly. "Thy faith shall be rewarded. And for thy servant, I would say, God hath given, and shall give."

The dumb youth knelt quickly and would have kissed his feet; but Merlin prevented him.

"Peace, I have not finished," he said; then whispered low, "I would say rather, God shall give if thou wilt receive."

The youth stood upright, and made no further effort to do the magician homage. His face was sternly set.

"Come, my servant Sanslangue," cried Ulfius importantly. "The damosel waits, and with her our adventure."

The youth followed obediently. The damosel's palfrey was ready, and also the two horses upon which the dwarf and his attendant had ridden to court. Amid many jests from the onlookers, and much laughter, the three were at last mounted and off. The damosel, sulky and speechless, rode first, then the dwarf, and finally the dumb youth.

"If thou dost come to evil pass," cried after them one laughing knight, "depend on thy servant, Ulfius, rather than on thy own prowess. That shield, methinks, is better fitted to his arm than thine."

Neither Ulfius nor the damosel replied. They crossed the drawbridge, and traversed in leisurely fashion the winding way that led out upon the high road. Merlin stood watching them until at length they were out of sight.

"On what dreamest thou, Uncle Merlin?" inquired the jester, affectionately snuggling up to him.

"I think on how the Black Art made fools of king and court," answered Merlin calmly. "I wonder whether the dwarf learned it among the Saracens."

The sunset glow had faded and the mists were rising as the damosel and her attendants reached at length the high road. As they passed the rose-bower near the gateway, the mute turned and looked toward it. The others did not see the movement, for he rode last. There among the roses, dim in the dim light, clad in gray, the color of the mists that rose about her, stood Dieudonnée de Cameliard, the queen's waiting-woman. The dumb servant had an instant's fleeting wonder whether it were verily a damosel, or some enchantment of Morgan le Fay. She stood there quite still, her great eyes mysterious, appealing, her golden hair dead in the dusk of twilight. The mute bowed his head, and thrust his hand within his bosom. There was an instant's flutter of blue samite. Then of a sudden nothing was visible save the gray mists rising from the gray earth.

CHAPTER THREE

In • The • Rosebower • • •

The thick white dust rose in clouds behind the three riders as they passed along the high road at a brisk trot. They kept now almost abreast, the mute guiding and controlling the led horses. At last they entered a by-path through the woods. The trees meeting overhead made a night so black that a man must trust for safety to the instincts of his steed.

The dumb servant was scarcely conscious of the country through which they passed, for his thoughts were lingering in the rose-bower. Unmindful of his present master, of the lady who was their leader, of the quest on which they were bound, he painted on the darkness round about a picture which for twice twenty-four hours had filled his mind, and which was the reason for his present adventure.

He saw the gardens of Camelot, not enwrapped by mists of evening, but resplendent with brilliant sunshine. Like flowers seemed the fair ladies, arrayed in their gayest in honor of the roses; and the roses—had sweeter ones ever bloomed? They tempted all the lovers in Arthur's court of lovers, and he with the rest searched joyously for the best and the most beautiful flowers to gather for his lady. Dully now he remembered his delight when, deciding at last that he could hold no more, he passed through the bright throng to find those white hands which would receive his offerings. He had been greeted with many merry jests as he went, and responded lightheartedly in kind. His joy was too perfect to be marred by ridicule.

When at last he knelt before her, his heart throbbed at her thanks, her exclamation of pleasure.

"But I cannot carry all," she said, smiling down at him.

She paused an instant, then went on, suiting the action to the word with rapid graceful fingers. "See! I shall twine some in my hair—thus; and these fair blossoms shall form a girdle for me. Ah, there are so many. Behold!" Then on the instant, it seemed to him, she stood a dream lady, an enchantment, an embodied rose. Roses encircled her neck and waist, and twined in her golden hair. From her bosom their sweetness breathed, and they fell fragrantly adown the long lines of her gown. All the white blossoms she gathered into her blue samite scarf, and held them in her arms.

"My lady of roses!" he cried.

"Carry the rest," she said, "and come, Prince Anguish. See where the sunshine invites us, there yonder on the pleasance; and here, nearby, the shadows of this wooded path are no less grateful. Come."

Her bright smile invited him as much as her words and the sunshine. He sprang to his feet gayly, and offered her his hand. Away they strayed, over the green lawns and along the forest paths, joying in the day and in their youth.

The afternoon passed quickly. The king and queen left at last to go to the evening service, and little by little the gardens were deserted. The Vesper bells began to chime as the two lingered in the rose-bower.

The castle lay gray in the distance, dark against the sunset clouds. The youth clasped his hands before the roses in his arms and said his prayers. As he did so, his eyes upon her, it were hard to tell whether his Angelus were recited for her, or to her. Our Lady, my lady, the two were one in his thought.

When the chimes had died away, she spoke.

"What peace is here!" she said. Her tone caused a sudden chill in his heart. As she moved forward, he dropped his wealth of flowers, and held out his hands beseechingly.

"Dear lady," he said, "tarry here but a little longer with me."

She paused at his words, and leaned over the back of the stone bench, covered with climbing roses. This lady, sad and silent, seemed no longer his fair companion of the afternoon, all youth and sunshine. Motionless she stood there, and he moved no nearer. He could not understand what stayed him, but he feared lest the clear look in her eyes might check the words on his lips.

"Dieudonnée," he whispered low at last, "Dieudonnée, I love thee."

She did not move, and there was a moment's pause. At length she answered low:

"O silly boy!"

What had she meant? he cried within himself, driving his horse forward with a sudden movement and gazing with unseeing eyes at the dark road, as he reached this point in his recollections. Boy! and my years outnumber hers. Had I been a tiny child, a toddling babe, her tone could scarce have been more chiding or more tender. So might she speak to a son; but to a lover—he remembered the moment's shock, his quick step forward to see her face. At the same time, she moved again in the direction of the castle. Her eyes were very calm.

"Let us go, Prince Anguish," she said.

"My answer first I crave," he said with a brave front, though fearful of he knew not what.

"Thou hast heard it."

"'Twas no answer," he said, "from a lady to her knight."

"Soothly?" she replied, somewhat wearily; "but here is neither knight nor lady. I am not the lady for thee, and thy spurs are yet to win, Prince Anguish."

Impetuously he knelt before her.

"Dieudonnée," he said, "God-given! The day I stood first before the throne with the king my father, and was welcomed by Arthur to his court, mine eyes met thine, and then—Prythee accept my love and my service! Dieudonnée, Dieudonnée, is not the gift of thy dear self for me?"

She had neither encouraged nor repulsed him by word or gesture. He seized both her hands and covered them with kisses, while she spoke quietly though tremulously after his passionate outburst.

"Prince Anguish," she began, and paused. Her voice was ever low and deep, inscrutable as her eyes. "Anguish, thou dost know me not, and yet anguish knows me, soothly, soothly."

"I love thee," he said again. "My lady thou art, and dear, and wilt be always. Knight I am not yet, nor have I ridden like Galahad and Percivale, in quest of the Holy Grail. But the day cometh soon, when for God and my lady, I ride forth into the world; and when my giants all are slain and my guerdon won; when I have seen the Vision—"

"Thou dost deceive thyself," she said, interrupting him somewhat harshly.

It was growing darker and the stars were coming. One, bright and solitary, shone just above them. Looking up at it, he breathed a prayer for this dear lady whom he knew so little yet so greatly loved. The white roses she had carried lay scattered on the ground. Her blue samite scarf had fallen unheeded beside them. He lifted it and pressed it to his lips.

"Wilt give it me," he said, "that I may wear it as thy favor?"

There was an instant's pause. Then she answered slowly. "Since thou askest, I suffer thee to have it, but when thou dost regret,—remember I warned thee."

He seized her hand and kissed it. It lay passively in his grasp.

"O Lady of Anguish," he said, "I shall not long delay the winning of my high reward. To-morrow, I will to the king, and go to seek such adventures as he may suggest or command. See, here shall lie thy scarf, close folded above that heart where thou dwellest ever enshrined, God-given and beloved."

He had taken her hand to lead her to the castle, and found her trembling greatly. What emotion had he aroused by his impetuous wooing? He tried to recall each word and look. When they had passed the great gateway, he stayed her.

"Dearest lady, methinks my words have troubled thee—"

She loosened the roses from her hair and dress before she replied. The petals had fallen and the leaves drooped. She watched them with sad eyes while they fell to the ground; then, as she held the last spray in her hand, she spoke, gazing upon it.

"When thou didst bring me them, Prince Anguish, they were sweet and fresh, indeed the fairest thou couldst find. Now they are faded. I fear me the love of which thou hast spoken so fervently will perish also, being like these without root. Nay," as he would have spoken in protest, "thou know'st me not nor understand'st. Yet perchance," and her voice quickened into bitter gayety, "I may adorn the June afternoon of thy life, and when thy quest is won and the victor's crown is on thy brow, thou may'st cast me aside as neither sweet nor dear. When the scarf is torn and faded, throw it to the winds, and let them carry it away out of sight and memory."

She let fall the withered spray, but he snatched it ere it reached the ground. Love is wise, and like a divining-rod discovers hid treasures. He goes not wrong who trusts it.

"I love thee," he said again, "I love thee truly. Heaven keep thee safe till I return. I shall protect thee from mischance and woe, and guard thee forever, my God-given."

"Farewell," she answered low, "farewell. God bless thee—now and always."

She had gone to the queen's apartments, and he had sought Arthur and received permission to go forth to win his spurs. Afterwards he had walked through the moon-lit gardens to the rose-bower. He had kept the withered spray, for it had trailed over Dieudonnée's gown from her girdle to her feet, and he could not cast it away. In the rose-bower at length, beside the bench where she had sat, he loosened the earth and planted the spray, banking it securely.

Sad and fearful, with chill forebodings at his heart, he had wandered restlessly all that night. Early next morning, Arthur having granted him leave to travel, Anguish left the court without farewell. Making a detour through the orchards, he reached the spot where he had planted the rose-branch the night before. The leaves had fallen off, but a delicate bud was upon it half open.

"Ah, Dieudonnée, dear and cruel lady," he said, "if this be the symbol of my love, it will not perish, for the branch has taken root."

And with lighter heart, he had turned to meet unexpectedly face-to-face, Ulfius the dwarf, ancient servant of his house.

CHAPTER FOUR

Guenever's Chamber

Guenever the queen leaned listlessly against the lattice in her chamber at Camelot. A woman waved a great fan before her, for the day was warm. A minstrel sang, softly touching his harp.

"Ah, love, 'tis the spring;
Thou art mine;
 Hark the birds, how they sing;
I am thine.

'Ah, sweet, summer comes;
Thou art mine; Every passing bee hums,
I am thine.

'Ah, heart, the leaves die;
Thou art mine; Weal or woe, smile or sigh,

I am thine.

'Ah, dear, snows are cold;
Thou art mine; Death is come, love is old;
I am thine."

At the song's close, Guenever moved impatiently.

"Why sing of sorrow and winter and the grave in June?" she cried petulantly. "Thou sour minstrel! Look without, and see how the green earth and the sweet roses rebuke thy doleful ballad. Dieudonnée, give him a piece of gold, and bid him hence. Next time, seek me, fellow, with a more cheerful lay."

Dieudonnée moved obediently from her place behind the queen, and did as she was told. The minstrel bowed his thanks, and left the room. A few moments later, they saw him cross the court-yard and walk down the winding path that led to the free country that lay beyond. Dieudonnée looked after him with a strange wistfulness in her gaze. She did not share in the laughing chatter of the other women, to whom either a coming or departing guest was a welcome break in the monotony of their lives. Guenever noticed her silence, and it seemed to fit with the queen's own mood.

"Enough!" she cried, lifting her hands against the Babel. "I weary of your tongues, and would be alone. Go into the outer chamber with your tapestry, damosels, all save Dieudonnée."

The bevy streamed forth obediently, not without some meaning glances backward, and many low-toned jealous whispers, beneath the upper chorus of gay chatter. Finally, as the curtains fell behind the last of the group, Guenever sighed and stood upright, stretching her arms high above her head.

"Now I may rest me for a little space," she cried. "They are well sped. Tell me, Dieudonnée, of what thou wert thinking a while since when thou didst gaze out after that minstrel."

Dieudonnée shrugged.

"Soothly, dear lady," she answered quietly, "I cannot say. Thoughts are roving things. One scarce can chain them."

Guenever pouted. "I am sure thou must know," she began coaxingly; then with a sudden flash of anger, "I command! Tell me thy thought."

Dieudonnée looked up at the queen's petulant face with a glint of mockery in her eyes.

"I yield me," she said resignedly; then she turned towards the lattice, and spoke with passion, as if to herself alone, "I thought how sweet a thing it was—ah, Jesu, how sweet!—to ride forth into the June, free, free, with only a song for company, and a pure heart."

Guenever looked puzzled. "Nay," she said, "methinks rather it were joy to ride home again—to love." She stretched out yearningly her white arms towards the lattice. "Ah, Launcelot!" she scarcely breathed.

Dieudonnée looked at her gravely. The queen was beautiful indeed, as she stood before the open window, her tall figure outlined against the summer sky beyond. Her coronet of raven hair proclaimed her sovereignty rather than circlet of gold. The dark eyes at once challenged and besought.

"Ah, Launcelot!" breathed the queen again. Then she turned and looked sharply at Dieudonnée. "Thou knowest?" she said, half fearfully, half defiantly.

"Ay," replied Dieudonnée, gazing at her with neither dread nor disapproval. The queen stood uncertain for an instant, then with a sudden smile she went and gathered Dieudonnée in her arms.

"I love thee," she whispered. "I love thee well. Thou art of Cameliard, my birthplace, and for that I love thee as well as for thyself. Let us now talk of Cameliard, Dieudonnée—Cameliard, where I was young —and innocent—and happy—"

Her voice trembled, and the tears rushed into her eyes. Dieudonnée stood, submitting passively to the queen's embrace. A maiden of ice could scarce have been less responsive.

"Soothly?" she said calmly in reply to the queen's last words. "But were those days so happy then? Happier than these—with love and Launcelot?"

The queen started away from her.

"Dieudonnée!" she cried, somewhat breathlessly; and crossed herself. "Is sin ever happiness?"

"The priests say not," said Dieudonnée.

"The priests say sooth," said Guenever, and even as she spoke her eyes turned yearningly towards the lattice.

"The priests!" repeated Dieudonnée bitterly. "A priest cursed me. He may have been quite right. Natheless, I hate all priests for his sake."

She paused abruptly, having spoken rather to herself than to the queen. But Guenever had not heard.

She cast the lattice wide, and leaned far out. Her head was uplifted, her eyes desirous, her lips parted in a smile.

Dieudonnée looked at her an instant; then made a quick step forward. The next moment, Guenever started to behold a face close to hers, wide eyes fastened upon her with a compelling gaze.

"Tell me," said Dieudonnée, "tell me, when Sir Launcelot is here, does aught matter? Does sin, does discovery—nay, does God?"

Guenever, with a frightened cry, sought to draw back into the chamber. Dieudonnée's arm was thrown lightly across behind her, and the barrier, though slender, was firm. The steady questioning blue eyes, sombre, infinitely calm, compelled the shifting dark ones.

"Tell me," said Dieudonnée again.

"Naught matters," Guenever answered, as if under a spell.

Dieudonnée's eyes left the queen's, and looked out dreamily over the fair June earth.

"I wonder," she said, "whether that is love."

Her arm fell and the queen sprang back released. She stood, trembling, offended. Dieudonnée turned from the window and looked at Guenever quietly. There was an instant's silence.

"Summon hither my maidens," said Guenever at length, rather tremulously.

As the last damosel left the ante-room, Dieudonnée slipped between the curtains and into the hallway. A little later, a slender gray figure passed the guards, and entered the great forest that stretched behind the Castle of Camelot.

CHAPTER FIVE

erlin's • Oak • •

Merlin sat among the shadows of the forest beneath a great oak, hooded, motionless, a figure of fate. Dieudonnée paused by a tree just beyond, and stood looking at him a moment.

There was absolute silence for a space; the stillness of a forest where no birds sing, and where no breeze is stirring. Then a twig snapped beneath Dieudonnée's foot. Merlin did not start, but he turned his head slowly towards her. She felt that he was looking at her, although she could not see his eyes. His cowl-like hood was pulled so far over his face that no features were visible.

"Welcome, thou Dryad of the Birch-tree," said Merlin's deep voice at length. "I know thee who thou art; for thou standest there against thy home. Moreover, thy garments are gray, like the tree thou lovest; and the green shadows are about thee—"

Dieudonnée laughed.

"Nay," she observed, coming forward and calmly seating herself opposite Merlin. "Thy words are as a minstrel's, Merlin but no dryad am I. Look well! Thou knowest me."

"Ay, soothly. Thou art Dieudonnée de Cameliard," the magician answered.

"Oh, wise Merlin!" said Dieudonnée sweetly. "Soothly I am that Dieudonnée, God-given or devil given, I know not which."

"One day thou wilt know," said Merlin quietly, keeping his steady gaze upon her.

"A safe saying," answered Dieudonnée. "I doubt me not I shall—but when and where? Tell me, Merlin, thou who dost know so much. When and where? The priests would say at death, in hell—but thou art no priest. Some say that thou art the devil's servant rather than God's. Come, show thy power. Read for me my fate."

She clasped her hands lightly about her knees as she sat at his feet, and smiled up at him with an air of challenge.

"Thou art of Cameliard," answered Merlin dreamily, "but rather, in sooth, thou art not of Cameliard, nor of England, nor of to-day, nor yesterday, nor to-morrow. To other damosels in good time the knight, and the love-token, and marriage, and child-bearing; so their life, and at the end, a happy death. But to thee—"

His voice sank into sudden silence.

Dieudonnée sat gazing at him steadily. She was very pale, but the smile of challenge still lingered on her lips.

"To me?" she repeated.

Merlin sighed. "I cannot tell—yet. Some day."

"Ay, when my fate has chanced," she said. "Art thou' then a cheat, a lie, O wise man, like all the rest?"

Merlin was silent. Dieudonnée leaned forward, and with a quick movement flung back the cowl from his head, and exposed his face. He looked at her still unmoved. His silver hair fell, a shaggy mass, about his pale face. His eyes, which now showed little color but the black, saw shapes and scenes not within the range of other mortals' ken.

"Awake, thou dreamer," said Dieudonnée, as calm as he; "awaken to the day! Tell me now the truth. Thou canst not deceive me."

Still Merlin did not speak. His hands had been folded in his gown. Now he withdrew one slowly, and reached it upward until it touched Dieudonnée's. Dauntless in spirit, her body was sometimes taken by surprise; and as Merlin's clammy fingers met hers she gave an involuntary shiver. The next instant she clasped his hand firmly. With a compelling touch, still in silence, he drew her quietly, gradually close beside him. His eyes were fixed upon her, his death-like hand clasped hers, slender and beautiful.

The subdued green light seemed to assume a threatening look, sinister, mysterious. Dieudonnée, gazing into Merlin's eyes, felt rather than saw the air grow dark, the atmosphere breathless. Even as she looked the wizard was no longer there. Great clouds of greenish smoke enveloped her so thickly that she saw not even the trees. It was as if she were alone on some isolated point, far from the ken of man. She was conscious of nothing save the insistent touch of Merlin's hand on hers.

Gradually, as she gazed into the misty space, it cleared, or, rather, resolved itself into definite shape. She saw again the rose-bower, and young Anguish kneeling at her feet. Herself she beheld with a curious feeling, as if looking at her own soul embodied. She saw the Irish prince kissing the hem of her samite scarf, and bending above him her own face, convulsed with a strange mixture of emotions. Still looking, she saw gradually forming behind the pair an ominous shape, dark, threatening, the figure of a man, with features indistinct. She gazed and trembled, striving her utmost to see his face. Then of a sudden it became clear. The head turned, the eyes looked, not towards the Dieudonnée of the vision, but upon her very self. She gave a shriek, and at the sound the figures melted immediately into wavering mist-clouds.

While the green vapors formed once again into definite outlines, Dieudonnée stood trembling. She looked fearfully at last, and recognized the winding way that led from the castle to the high road; and down it, passing slowly, the three steeds that bore the damosel, the dwarf, and the dumb servant. The mute, riding last, turned and looked, as he had looked that evening, at the rose-bower. As he did so his head-covering fell back, and disclosed the ardent face of Anguish of Ireland.

"I knew," said Dieudonnée; "I knew." And at the words the vision melted as before.

"Is it enough?" she heard Merlin's deep voice say beside her. She turned, but, straining her eyes, could not see him. She was trembling now from head to foot; but her invincible will stood firm.

"Nay," she answered and although her voice shook, it still mocked. "The future—I have not seen the future."

She thought she heard a sigh.

"O child," said Merlin's voice at length, "child, seek no more. I love thee well, for thou art of the few through the ages who sound the depths and reach the heights. Wait. Seek not to read the future."

"I do not fear," said Dieudonnée. "It cannot be more bitter than the past."

Merlin did not reply. She gazed again at the green mists, and saw them forming into shape. The hour and place of the last vision were not clear. She saw only Anguish and herself, standing together at some strange point where space and time counted nothing. Her hands were clasped in grief, her eyes a prayer of pain. But Anguish's head was turned away, his attitude repelled, his face spoke scorn. Between them lay at their feet a blue samite scarf, the sword of Anguish, and a withered rose.

Dieudonnée looked with neither word nor sound, looked for one long moment. Then the outraged body rebelled at last. She sank prone of a sudden, as if stabbed to the heart, and Merlin knelt above a still gray figure beneath the great oak.

erlin sat among the shadows of the forest

CHAPTER SIX

The • Quest • of • Ulfius

Ulfius and the maiden rode forth into the June weather, and Sanslangue, the dumb servant, rode behind. The damosel treated the dwarf, for the most part, with haughty silence. Ulfius, quite unmoved by her scorn, talked cheerfully by turns of his native land, of the people they passed, of King Arthur and the knights of the Table Round. In return, he tried to obtain information on the subject of the girl's mistress and her sorry plight; but of both the damosel would say little.

"Wait until we reach the castle of my lady," she mocked. "That will try thy mettle, little man. I look to see thee, at sight of the giant, turn and gallop back to Arthur and his court; whither I will follow thee to obtain a fitter champion."

Once they had converse with Sir Palomides the Saracen, pursuing Galtisant, the Questing Beast. He spent a night with them in the forest, and told them of the creature he followed. Headed like a serpent it was, he said, with a body like a leopard, and footed like a hart. The noise it made was like unto the baying of thirty couples of hounds. Sir Palomides, a gallant knight, heard with wonder of the adventure, and looked doubtfully at the height and bulk of Ulfius. He did not express his thought however; and in this he was more considerate than the next knight they encountered, Sir Breuse Sans Pité, who laughed when he heard what adventure was toward, and at once challenged the dwarf to combat.

"Let us end the matter," he said. "I will run thee through, little man, and so rid this fair damosel of that which she desires not. Then I will myself take up thy adventure, and go to rescue that fair lady."

"Nay, not so," replied the dwarf unmoved. "This is my own adventure, an it please thee, Sir Breuse, bestowed upon me by King Arthur. I will not lightly give it up for thee nor any man. Nor will I fight thee; for I have sworn an oath to encounter no knight until I have achieved my quest."

Sir Breuse laughed again, and went his way. The damosel looked after him with longing.

"There goes a knight indeed," she cried, passionately. "Ah, thou craven, how I wish he had run thee through, that I might bear a more fitting savior to my lady!"

"Thou wilt not so lightly lose me," Ulfius replied, placidly.

At last, seven days and seven nights had worn away; and on the eighth morning at dawn they reached the castle that they sought. Rose-red soared its turrets, and the rose glow of dawn was behind it.

"Red," said Ulfius, importantly to the damosel, "red is the color of love—and likewise of sin. Doubtless it speaks the former here, as thy lady shall know after I have won her. Where skulks this giant, that the affair may be concluded at once?"

The damosel halted her palfrey.

"Here I leave thee," she said. "Farewell, runtling, and God on thy soul have mercy, for I shall not see thee alive again, A little way straight onward, and thou wilt be met by the giant. Farewell."

She blew him a mocking kiss, and spurred her palfrey. Ulfius sat on his horse motionless, watching until she had disappeared behind a clump of trees opening into a forest. Then he turned to Sanslangue.

"What sayest thou?" he said. "Have I done the business well for thee? This chances luckily. I wondered oft how we could rid ourselves of her when the time came."

"Thou hast well played thy part, thou good servant," answered Sanslangue. "Change places now. Later, if all goes well, thou shalt be, perchance, once again master, and I servant. Now my work must be done. Come into the forest."

Ulfius followed him obediently. A little later the two emerged upon the high road. Sanslangue's cloak and hood, in a close-packed bundle, were tied to the saddle of the horse that the mute had been riding. The dwarf was still in rich attire; but his sword hung by Sanslangue's side. The dumb servant was clad in full armor. He vaulted into the saddle of Ulfius's horse; then paused an instant, and clasped his hands as if in prayer.

"Dieudonnée!" he breathed. "O Jesu, for her and the Holy Grail!" And it did not occur to him, as he struck spurs into his horse, that he had mentioned his lady first in his prayer.

They rode a few rods further in dead silence. Nothing was to be heard save the low rustle of the leaves, the soft twitter of the newly-awakening birds. His senses were so enraptured with the beauties about him that almost his mission had been forgotten, when a hoarse roar awoke him from his day-dream. The next instant a huge creature, half again the height of an ordinary man, stood astride the pathway, confronting them. The young man did not turn his head, but he called back to the dwarf.

"Stay thou there, Ulfius," he cried, "and if I should fall, go thou to the Lady Dieudonnée, and tell her that she is ever in life and death the lady of my heart."

"God speed thee, Prince Anguish!" cried Ulfius in reply.

The giant gave another roar. Anguish closed his visor on the instant, and feutred his spear. The giant was also fully armed and he raised his spear with a shout. The two met fairly. They reeled from the shock, but neither fell.

"Well done!" cried Anguish gayly, drawing his sword. "Now let our combat end speedily."

The ill-matched pair came close. The giant smote Anguish a great wound in the side; but Anguish seemed not to feel either wound or pain. The two lashed eagerly with their swords, and the dwarf, watching them from under the trees, beheld them hurtling together, tracing and traversing, for a great space of time. At last, after more than two hours' combat. Anguish swung high his sword, and with a mighty effort, drove it clean through the waist of the giant, so straight and fast that it was needful to pull the weapon thrice, or ever he could draw it forth again.

The giant gave one great groan, and died. Anguish stood panting, the blood streaming. Ulfius hastened towards him. As he did so he saw several women's figures watching on the walls of the castle. An instant later the damosel, who had brought them thither, came running at full speed towards them.

"The lady thou hast rescued sends to thank thee, master," he said; but Anguish did not hear. He was drunk with the joy of victory and he dreamed of Dieudonnée.

The damosel came nearer, reached them.

"Well fought, my lord!" she cried, as soon as she came within speaking distance. "My lady sends you thanks and blessing, and beseeches that you will come into her castle as her guest to rest you of your wounds and to receive her benison and reward."

"I am well pleased to do so, damosel," responded Anguish, courteously. Then of a sudden his voice failed him. The fair morn, flushed with victory, grew black. He fell upon the grass in a deep swoon.

It was on a litter borne between Ulfius and the maiden that Anguish, the conqueror, entered unconscious the castle of the besieged lady.

CHAPTER SEVEN

The Castle of Hellayne • •

Anguish awoke slowly, dreamily aware of an atmosphere of heavy perfume lapping his drowsy senses. He lifted one arm languidly; it moved stiffly, and he saw that it was bandaged. He had not sufficient strength in his throbbing body to turn his head; but as he gazed upward at the roof, he saw that he was in the great hall of a castle. Gradually memory returned, but somewhat vaguely, and with a certain torment. He had fought, he had been wounded, he had conquered, but why? The thought annoyed him, and at last, with a sigh, he strove to raise himself. There was a quick rustle of silken garments, and he saw a woman's face bending above him.

"Rest thee still, my lord," said a voice gently; "thou art not yet healed of thy wounds obtained in my behalf."

Following close upon the solicitous words. Anguish heard a somewhat distant peal of mocking laughter. The face bending above him flushed with annoyance, and the lady stood upright with a frown. But Anguish comfortably closed his eyes. Bodily content shut out for the time all thought. With a long sigh, he straightway fell asleep.

The lady beside him stood watching him with an expression of mingled triumph and dread. Her thoughts were interrupted by a light footfall. She looked up, again frowning slightly, and saw the damosel of the golden shield standing before her. The maiden was smiling with an air of mockery.

"I await your future orders, Lady Hellayne."

"I have none," answered her mistress, "save the old one—that the dwarf be kept away from him and that we be left alone together till he awakes. Afterwards —" She paused, and a smile touched her lips.

Anguish was lying on a couch made on the dais at the head of the hall. As the damosel reached the doors at the opposite end, and opened them, Ulfius the dwarf put an anxious face into the aperture.

"How fares he?" he whispered, softly, anxiously.

"He still sleeps," the maiden answered. "Come away. He is in the hands of my mistress."

"May I not see him?" asked the dwarf pleadingly. "I have not been near him since we carried him into the castle yesterday. Let me go to him, good damosel. None has a better right. I have been his plaything, his slave, since his birth. His father rescued me from the Saracens, who kept me in tortured slavery—"

He bared an arm, horribly scarred with old wounds. "From that his father saved me," he said; "and so I am his dog, and his son's, for ever. Let me see him, damosel."

The maiden closed the doors carefully behind her.

"Thou may'st well love King Marhalt and Prince Anguish," she said, looking at the dwarf narrowly.

"Prince Anguish?" he repeated questioningly. "What meanest thou, damosel?"

The maiden laughed.

"Why has this foolery of dwarf and dumb servant been played on me?" she said sharply. They were walking along the corridor, side by side.

"That, damosel," replied Ulfius, "that I shall keep to myself, until my master bids me speak."

"Then, dog, thou shalt not see thy master, until thou hast told me," cried the damosel. She gave the dwarf a smart box upon the ears, and laughed. Ulfius looked at her gravely.

"Why dost thou mock me, damosel?" he said. "Thou knowst us for what we are, master and servant. The jest is ended."

"Nay, the jest begins, if thou didst but know it," the maiden cried, and flung herself away from him, still laughing. Ulfius looked after her, knitting his brows.

"There is something here I cannot fathom," he said reflectively. "Methinks I like not the air of this castle. I wonder—she did not lock the doors."

There was no one near. Ulfius turned and walked thoughtfully back to the doors of the great hall. He tried them cautiously, and found them, to his joy, unlocked. He opened them, inch by inch, stealthily, and at last peered in.

He saw the mistress of the castle kneeling beside the couch on the dais. Her back was towards the doors. Ulfius pushed them open a little further and slipped through. The arras hung a convenient distance from the wall to afford him concealment. He crept behind it, and looked out anxiously. He thought he saw a movement upon the couch. An instant, and Anguish sat waveringly upright. At the same moment, Hellayne rose.

"Thou art rested, and thy wounds are soothed, O my hero!" Ulfius heard her say.

Anguish put his hand to his head, and looked at her searchingly, uncertainly. Hellayne fell upon her knees, and clasped her hands.

"Thy wounds are healed," she said. "It is time now that thou shouldst heal mine."

Anguish looked uncomprehending as Hellayne took his hand in hers.

"Prince Anguish!" she whispered. "Ah, Anguish, Prince of Ireland, thou art come to me at last!"

Anguish made no attempt to withdraw his hand. He gazed at her still in mute inquiry.

"Dost wonder that I know thy name, Prince Anguish?" she said. "I ken things in ways that others do not; for I was once a maiden of Morgan le Fay. I saw thee—from a room in this castle—I saw thee—it is now nigh two months—thou with thy father didst leave thy home and cam'st towards Arthur's court. How eagerly I watched that lad flinging his challenge defiantly and fearlessly to all who opposed or thwarted him! I loved that youth who rode through the forest and sailed over the seas with his heart full of dreams and his soul all courage. The boy is man now—he came to his own in Arthur's court—and I love the man as the youth."

Anguish started. A faint flush crept over his face, and he drew his hand from hers. He wavered for an instant, then fell prone again. Hellayne, kneeling beside him, leaned far over the couch, and brought her face close to his. Her perfumed hair swept his cheek. Her sinuous body almost touched his own.

"I love thee, Anguish," she repeated, and her voice was low and passionate. "Prythee, deny me not. I knew that thou wouldst desire to go on a quest, so I made this quest for thee. I knew that thou wouldst come, but sorely did thy servant Ulfius perplex my messenger at the court. That giant was my leal guardian, and did never persecute me. When the dwarf came as thy lord, I bade the giant slay him, and bring thee hither; but thou didst ride against the monster, and, not understanding, he strove to kill thee. Natheless, thou art here, thou art mine. It is enough. Ah, my love, my love!"

Anguish looked up at her, his face pale, his eyes staring. He strove to speak, and could not. His brain was awhirl with thoughts and memories that he strove to hold, yet felt them slipping fast away. Hellayne threw herself upon his breast, and wreathed her white arms about his neck.

"Anguish, Anguish," she whispered, and yet again.

Anguish shut his eyes. Memory receded, was lost in the present. Hellayne laid her cheek against his, and drew his arms around her slender body.

A sudden heart-broken cry broke across the perfumed stillness of the hall. Ulfius the dwarf rushed from behind the tapestry and up to the dais.

"Master, master," he cried, raising beseeching hands; "master, remember Dieudonnée! Thou art her knight in life and death. Remember Dieudonnée!"

Hellayne, a voiceless fury, drew a dagger from her girdle and stabbed the dwarf to the heart. He sank dead without a groan. The deed accomplished, Hellayne looked fearfully at Anguish. But Anguish had neither heard nor seen. He lay with closed eyes in a strange stupor, so far away that even the name of Dieudonnée could not bring him back to life.

CHAPTER EIGHT

Arthur's hunting.

The horses were ready, and the court prepared to go a-hunting. Knights and ladies, pages and damosels jostled each other, chattering gaily, a bright throng. Guenever, all in dark green, a vivid red rose just below her white throat, sat stately upon her horse. Near her, Dieudonnée de Cameliard, pale and still, held the reins listlessly, and gazed dreamily out upon the winding road that led from Camelot to the open country. Sir Kaye the Seneschal, bustling hither and yon, was arranging matters in general, seeing every one horsed, and putting the cavalcade into proper order of rank.

At length all was ready. The king swung into his saddle, a goodly man with yellow hair and beard glistering in the sunlight. A moment later, and, winding down from Camelot, the hunting party was away.

Dagonet the jester, riding in and out of the gay throng and leaving here a laugh and there a sting, reached at length Dieudonnée de Cameliard, and pulled his mule into step with her horse.

"Damosel! Lady Dieudonnée! Here we ride, two fools together!"

She started and smiled, faintly and half mockingly.

"It is the wise man who knows that he is a fool. Thou speakest sooth," she said, humoring him, and looked away.

"I have not seen thee this sennight," the jester went on. "I have been on a quest with my good knight and uncle. Merlin, the only one who can raise me from my lowly estate of squire to the lofty rank of knight. But he has not yet done so; and I am still the jester, not the sage. Strange adventures seeks he in dark forests. I am glad to be in the sunlight with the hunt to-day—" and he caroled a merry song.

Dieudonnée went a shade paler at the mention of Merlin's name; but she made no reply. Dagonet looked at her keenly, and continued half complainingly.

"She rides alone; herself the noblest company in this noble company. *De mondo non est secut et ego non sum de mond*, as our ghostly fathers say. Like the fool, like the fool!" With a merry jingle of bells he made his mule plunge forward, but returning he scrutinized her impassive face. It was as if she had heard nothing. "Ah, Dagonet," he continued, pacing again by her side, and shaking whimsically at his bauble an admonitory finger, "she's not the fool, and thou art—as she is usually."

"In sooth a wise saying, but perplexing—as life."

"Nay, my fair and gentle lady, would you but count me a friend, this puzzle could I quickly clear; and so a true friend in life solves life's problems. Uncle Merlin should have knighted thee sage." But she sighed.

The jester heard the quiet breath, despairing and final, and forthwith threw his bauble high in the air, and caught it again with a roar of laughter.

"O, merry world!" he cried. "O, merry world! The man to whom God gives forgets, and the God-given remembers. Alack! Lose thy memory, lady. Believe me, 'tis the only way. When I steal meat from the kitchen, I forget it at once, so that I can tell Sir Kaye naught of its whereabouts. Lose thy memory, prythee."

Dieudonnée looked at him questioningly, with a certain fear. Her eyes besought. The jester started to sing,

> "Why, yesterday, I loved thee well;
> But it is now to-day;
> Thou'rt fair indeed—and others too;
> Love walks a winding way."

"Live, love, lady, and forget! And so adieu, fellow fool.—Room, room for me beside my Uncle Arthur. Make way, friends, make way!"

He shook his head until the bells on his cap rang again, and an instant later took his place beside the king. Dieudonnée, musing, rode onward, solitary and in silence, her truant heart traveling far.

Presently the cavalcade entered the forest, and after they had gone a short distance Guenever reined her horse, and declared that she wearied of the chase, and would pursue it no further. Accordingly, a pavilion was pitched beside a mossy fountain, and the queen and her ladies dismounted. Leaving certain knights as guard, the others pressed onward with the king.

The fountain cast diamonds in the sunlight; and the queen's ladies fluttered about it, some singing, some chattering. Guenever herself sat upon the brink, and held out her slender hands that the spray might fall upon them.

"Ah, earth, how fair; ah, June, how sweet!" cried the queen at length, shaking the water-drops from her taper fingers. "On such a day, methinks, love should ride home to love, and parting and sorrow should be as evil dreams."

At that instant a horse's hoofs were heard pacing along the high road near by. The knights guarding the pavilion challenged the newcomer. The ladies heard their voices change from question to delight. Guenever sprang upward and stood beside the fountain, lips parted and hands clasped. A moment, and a tall knight, clad in white armor, his visor closed, came slowly towards the queen.

Guenever gave a little cry, quickly suppressed. The knight came and knelt before her. As he did so, he doffed his helmet.

"Sir Launcelot!" said the queen, breathing quickly, yet speaking in stately fashion, "Sir Launcelot, thou art welcome. Thou hast tarried long from court."

Sir Launcelot bent his bared head, and kissed her hand. He spoke low in reply, and only Dieudonnée de Cameliard beside the queen caught his words.

"I have been in many lands, dear lady, with many men. I have foughten many battles, but in my heart the worst; have been among many sinners, but deemed myself the villain of them all; have beheld many fair women; none, my queen, like thee; none like thee."

She looked at him, flattered, passionate, uncomprehending. The red rose at her throat fell to the ground. He picked it up and placed it on his helmet.

"There let it wither," he said, smiling somewhat sadly. "It shall not be cast away until I have done some good deed for its sake, and for my queen's."

At the words, Dieudonnée involuntarily clasped her hands. A moment, and Launcelot and Guenever began to pace up and down side by side, talking composedly. The eyes of the court were upon them; and whispers and nodding heads were plentiful. A few hours later, the king and his followers joined them, tired, but very joyous, since they had killed their hart. Arthur welcomed Launcelot with acclamation. It was near sunset now, and at the king's command the party made speedy preparations to return to Camelot.

"And there thou wilt tell us of thy adventures," Arthur said. "They must e'en be many. It is two years since thou hast gladdened our eyes at Camelot."

It chanced that for an instant Launcelot was left standing alone beside the fountain, while the hunting-party completed their final preparations. Dieudonnée looked at him, half in fear, half in hope, and went a step nearer.

"Sir Launcelot," she began, somewhat tremulously, "Sir Launcelot!"

He started and turned towards her. It was said that the heart of every maid and matron in England was at Sir Launcelot's feet. Dieudonnée could well believe it, as she looked on the stately figure, the kind, sad eyes, the face marred by the soul's long struggle with itself.

"What wouldst thou, damosel?" he said.

The queen's rose was drooping on his helmet.

"Thou bearest there a flower," said Dieudonnée, low but clearly, "and for its sake thou didst swear to perform a good deed. Lo, I crave a boon, Sir Launcelot, and as true knight thou wilt hear my prayer."

"Speak," he said simply.

"These many weary months," she said, in a low, controlled voice, "one Anguish of Ireland hath been gone from court. He went forth on a quest a year ago, and has never returned. Prythee—hast seen or heard aught of him in thy wanderings?"

She paused, panting a little. He looked at her with grave inquiry, but he asked no questions.

"I grieve, gentle maiden, for his friend's sake, that I must say nay. I know not Prince Anguish, but his father is a true knight, whom I have loved these many years. To-morrow, damosel, I shall ride forth to find whether ill hath beset him. I pray that ere this rose be brown I may return either with news of his achievements or with him."

CHAPTER NINE

The · Queen's · Rose · ·

The summer air breathed hot and languorous across the gardens of Hellayne. Lutes tinkled here and there. A plash of fountains made a perpetual accompaniment. Beneath the spreading branches of an apple-tree, Hellayne and Anguish sat, his arm thrown carelessly about her, she half reclining, with her head upon his breast.

"The summer is fair, my lord," she said. "June has come at last. There yonder on the terrace the roses are blooming; and in a sennight comes the Feast of Pentecost."

Anguish started at the word, and let her fall from his embrace somewhat roughly.

"Pentecost!" he muttered. "Pentecost!" He gave a short laugh of self-contempt, and looked away with gloomy eyes.

She put her arms about him and drew his cheek to hers. He did not return her embrace.

"I was to do a deed by Pentecost," he muttered; "by Pentecost; but now—"

"At Pentecost and at all times thou must love me," she murmured, touching his cheek with her lips. He drew himself away, and looked at her sadly.

"Thou hast wrecked my soul," he said. "And what hath it profited thee, lady?"

A horn was wound beyond the walls of the castle, and a moment later the damosel of the golden shield came running lightly across the grass to her mistress.

"Please thee, my lady," she cried, panting in her haste, "a stranger knight in white armor craves speech with thee. Methinks"—she lowered her voice—"methinks, from what I have heard men say and minstrels sing—it is no other than Sir Launcelot himself."

Hellayne started at the name and glanced involuntarily at Anguish. But Anguish had not heard. He had stretched himself under the apple-tree, and lay there a listless figure with closed eyes.

"I will see this stranger," answered Hellayne. "If he be indeed whom thou sayest—what rare sport it were to hear Guenever's name made a mock and in its high place Hellayne's. If that might be, then Anguish of Ireland might go whither he would. Having won him, I weary of him."

She went with the maiden. A moment later, the white knight, sitting motionless in his saddle with covered shield, saw upon the castle walls a slender woman clad in shining green like a serpent. She smiled and beckoned. He brought his steed within speaking distance.

"What will you, Sir Knight?" she asked.

"I am come hither, madam," he replied, "to demand that you deliver into my hands one Anguish of Ireland, whom ye have kept here this twelvemonth under your false spells."

Hellayne made a surprised gesture.

"Soothly, here is no knight of courtesy. What mean you sir? Anguish of Ireland is indeed my guest, but he is so willingly—"

"There thou speakest a foul lie," replied the knight calmly. "Bandy not words with me, Lady Hellayne. I know thee well, and all Arthur's court knows thee.

Thou hast lured hither many noble knights to their ruin. Deliver to me here Anguish of Ireland; and if thou dost refuse, I challenge whatever knight thou choosest to combat for him. Nay, if Anguish of Ireland be indeed thy willing guest, send him as thy champion."

Hellayne hesitated an instant. Then she gave a shrug.

"Even so. Run, damosel, arm Prince Anguish, and bring him hither."

A little later, Launcelot, sitting statue-like upon his horse, saw slowly mounting another steed a youth moving dully, as if careless what he did. The damosel of the golden shield aided him effusively, laughing meanwhile behind his back; and a dozen grinning serfs made japes at his appearance. Launcelot's heart burned within him at the sight. Mounted at last, his golden shield before him. Anguish took his spear, and feutred it listlessly.

Sir Launcelot called to him sharply. At the sudden cry, Anguish lifted his head, and seemed for the instant his old self. The two met with a crash, and the force of Sir Launcelot's blow sent Anguish's horse upon its knees. Anguish himself was thrown over its head, and lay an instant stunned.

Launcelot leaped from the saddle. He had done as he had intended; but he feared that he had perhaps done more.

"Anguish," he said imperatively, "Awaken! Bethink thee where thou art."

Anguish opened his eyes and sat up. Launcelot knelt beside him.

"Where hast thou been these long months, Prince Anguish? Thou didst ask the king to go forth on an adventure a year ago, and since then—"

Anguish looked at Launcelot, a deep shame, too accustomed longer to be wonder, present in his eyes.

Launcelot returned his gaze in speechless sorrow. Anguish sighed and rose.

"I thank you," he said. "Let us go hence, of your charity."

"To do that came I," said Launcelot gently. "Ere I left Arthur's court, I sought council of Merlin, and he told me—where thou art. Mount thy steed, and let us go. Thou hast dwelt in the castle of an evil sorceress; be not too cast down over thy fall. I will not take vengeance on Hellayne now. That I leave for thee to do later. Come. It is nigh the Feast of Pentecost, and they wait for us at Arthur's court."

As they rode together away from the castle of Hellayne, Launcelot unfastened from his helmet a withered rose, and dropping it gently, watched its petals flutter away on the breeze.

"The rose's work is done," he said; but sighed with the words.

CHAPTER TEN

In • the • Moonlight

Moonlight lay fair on Camelot, and Arthur's court, knights and ladies both, flocked out of doors in the sweet summer twilight. Launcelot and the queen sat by the fountain, and a minstrel sang before them. Arthur and Merlin walked the terrace, discussing affairs of state. Dagonet bounded from one group to another. Knights and ladies sat or strolled in pairs. The spell of the moonlight was on all.

Anguish of Ireland sat beneath a tree on the edge of the terrace, dark and remote from the rest. With folded arms and head bent moodily he looked out upon the scene where the chaste moon reigned over lawless love.

He made no attempt to join the rest, and he was for the most part unnoticed. He had returned to

Camelot the day before in company with Launcelot, and had met with little interest, since he brought no tale either of love or war to delight the ears of the court.

The golden shield, empty honor of a fool quest, he had with loathing covered, ere Launcelot and he had ridden a league from the castle of Hellayne. Now it stood in his room, a constant reproach, a constant mentor. He longed now only to leave the court and go back to Ireland. He would go back, back to his fair sister Isoud, who loved him well, and there perhaps forget—

His gloomy thoughts were interrupted by a jingle of bells, and Dagonet rushed up to him.

"The son of the King of Ireland!" he cried grimacing. He twisted his long legs into curious contortions. Finally, wreathing them comfortably, he seated himself before Anguish. "Why dost linger moping here? Behold where the moonlight calls men to love."

"Peace, fool," said Anguish, and threw him a coin. The jester caught it nimbly.

"I thank thee," he said. "For this pretty plaything's sake, I will hold peace indeed—but I could tell thee— prythee, another piece of gold!"

Anguish flung it to him, seeming half in anger.

"For both much thanks," said Dagonet, biting the coins cheerfully. "Come with me, Prince Anguish. 'Tis worth thy pains. These gold pieces are as twin gates which shall open happiness to thee."

"As well go with thee as anywhere," said Anguish bitterly, rising.

"Not together must we go through this honorable assemblage," said Dagonet, gazing at him reflectively. "Trust me, Prince. I have spoken sooth."

He pranced cheerfully down through the darkness of the orchard trees that bordered the terrace at its extreme end. Anguish followed indifferently; but after they had gone a short distance he realized whither the jester was leading him. He paused, and caught Dagonet by the ear.

"Another way!" he said imperatively. "What mean'st thou, varlet? I will not to the rose-bower."

"Well, if thou wilt not, thou wilt not," replied Dagonet, grimacing with the pain of his twisted ear. "But if thou dost not go thither, thou art not so wise as I." He rolled his eyes ecstatically.

Anguish released him. "Did any—send thee to seek me?" he asked, and his voice faltered.

"Ay," said Dagonet curtly, folding his arms and putting his head on one side.

Anguish shivered.

"It is well," he said, half aloud. "It must come, and now will be no more torture than another time. I understand, fellow. Get thee hence, and see that we are not disturbed."

Dagonet nodded, and sprang away. Anguish walked forward quickly a few paces, pushed aside the thorny branches that covered the entrance to the rose-bower, and went in.

She stood there waiting for him, as he had expected, clad in misty white like the moonbeams, her hands clasped lightly over her heart, her great eyes fathomless. He did not approach nearer, but stood just inside the entrance. So they waited in silence for an instant. Then she moved a step towards him.

"Wilt thou not speak to me?" she said.

"What can I say, lady?" he answered. "One word, indeed, fits my lips to thee, and that I shall speak, first beseeching thy pardon that ever I so wronged thee as to ask thy love for a weakling and a fool. It is—Farewell."

She was silent, motionless, her eyes upon his face.

"Dost know where I have been this twelvemonth?" he asked, smiling sombrely. "I am not fit to come nearer to thee, Dieudonnée, whom God after all gives not to me, but to one more worthy. Whoe'er he is, God him bless, and thee!"

He turned to leave her. She stayed him by a slight gesture of appeal.

"Wait," she breathed. "I said long since, Anguish, that thou dost not know me. Fear not to tell me all. Speak."

"Then briefly," he answered bitterly, "I went on a false quest, was lured by a fool guerdon. In bodily weakness, my soul was beguiled; and when I awoke to memory and shame, I found myself in the evil arms of a sorceress. There in self-loathing and despair have I lain this twelvemonth while other men fought and suffered and triumphed. Bears any knight of the Table Round such a record for his first adventure, tell me?"

"I know not," she said; "but this is not the end."

He stared at her miserably, uncomprehending. She went on in an even voice, but he saw that she trembled.

"If thou hadst come back aflush with victory," she said, "not knowing shame and defeat, thou couldst not have felt sympathy, temptation would have been to thee a name, sin a far-off thing, and love—a dream."

Her voice fell at the last word to its deepest note. He shook his head, not yet seeing her drift.

"I won the golden shield," he said between his teeth. "It stands covered in my room, a mockery. I shall never use it more."

"Say not so," she answered. "Thy years are not very many—yet." She smiled somewhat tremulously. "One day, thou wilt win honor for it and thee."

"That other woman stole my memory, my manhood," he went on doggedly; "how I scarce know yet; and afterwards, in despair, I lived in pleasure, in sin, in forgetfulness, so far as might be. Once I dreamed of achieving the Holy Grail. I!" He laughed in self-contempt.

"That yet may be," she said. He looked at her strangely.

"Thou dost pity me," he said. She smiled a little wistfully and shook her head.

"No, no." She paused, then added low and clear, "Only—thou dost look backward now. I would have thee look forward."

He gazed at her searchingly. Her eyes met his, unflinching. They were veiled, but they spoke infinite trust.

There was a long pause during which heart communed with heart.

At last Anguish stirred; but he could not trust his voice to speak the peace with which her sympathy had touched his wounded and sensitive spirit. Dropping on his knees, he pressed his lips reverently upon the hem of her dress; then rising, fled into the night, leaving her alone among the roses.

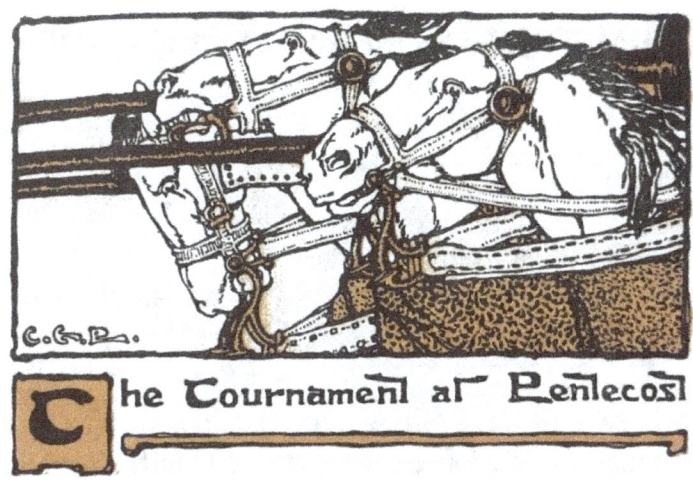

CHAPTER ELEVEN

The Tournament at Pentecost

The tournament of Pentecost was at its height. Full many brave knights had jousted each with other, and had conquered or been overcome, as fate and fortune chanced. Sir Launcelot had so far been victor in the field; and presently he left it and sought his place on the pavilion beside the king and queen, declaring himself weary. Arthur looked at him affectionately.

"Weary? Thou? Rather, methinks, thou wouldst give these younger knights opportunity. I know thee, Launcelot. Natheless, should none surpass thy record this day, the circlet of gold belongs to thee."

Launcelot bowed, and looked out across the field with dreamy, unseeing eyes. Success, being an old story, had grown somewhat stale. Presently his expression changed to intentness. He gazed for a moment, then leaned forward and spoke to the king.

"See yonder, Arthur. Another stranger knight approaches. These jousts attract full many."

A solitary knight rode slowly across the west end of the field, halted, consulted with Sir Kaye, and an instant later galloped toward the pavilion to salute the king; then turned to his place in the lists and awaited an opponent. His armor was black, his shield covered. Nothing about his habiliments betrayed his identity.

"Young by his carriage," said King Arthur; "but otherwise I can tell naught. He is, methinks, a stranger to our jousts. Let us try his mettle. See, Sir Gareth goes to meet him."

Sir Gareth and the stranger knight encountered with a crash, so hard that Sir Gareth was smitten straightway to the earth. Whereupon he rose and drew his sword, and the black knight dismounted likewise. Then they lashed together furiously a great while.

"Ne'er have I have seen two knights fight better," cried the king. "See, Launcelot, how the stranger knight doubles his strokes, and puts Gareth aback."

"He is young, but full noble," answered Launcelot. "None of the court better jousts than he."

The two knights ran together, and gave each other such buffets on the helm that they reeled backward. Then the stranger seemed to draw himself together as if to end the matter. He smote

Sir Gareth within the hand so that his sword fell out of it. Then he gave him another mighty blow upon the helm, and Sir Gareth fell groveling to the earth.

King and court rose to their feet with irrepressible enthusiasm, and with one accord called for the stranger knight. But ere Sir Kaye could reach him he mounted his horse, struck in his spurs, and galloped from the field.

"Alack!" cried the king disappointedly. "What have I lost? Jesu grant that one day he come again to the jousts, and that we find his name and station! Now that he is departed, the tournament will seem of little worth. Prythee, Launcelot, go again into the field."

"I beseech thee, hold me excused," answered Launcelot. "I have had my fill of jousting for this day."

"Now, by my Creator I am minded myself to try a fall," said the king. "Would that the black knight would return again, for so lusty a youngling I have not seen since Galahad came to court. What ho, Sir Kaye! Bring hither my horse and armor."

As the king left the pavilion Launcelot leaned towards Guenever.

"Prythee, my lady queen," he said in a low voice, "an you permit me, I would speak with a maiden of thine, one hight Dieudonnée de Cameliard."

The queen gave him a quick, jealous glance.

"Dost thou doubt me?" said Launcelot, smiling at her sadly. "Dost thou doubt me after all these years of faith? Ah, Guenever, surely I should have thy trust."

The queen, for answer, flushed, and beckoned to Dieudonnée. She came obediently, and bent over Guenever. She was very pale, and her great eyes looked black. Launcelot said to her quietly:

"There is a knight in green will appear on the field shortly that I would have thee well observe, damosel; and later one in red—"

The queen looked mystified. Dieudonnée's white face flushed into comprehension.

"I thank thee, Sir Launcelot," she answered in a low voice. "That knight in black, methinks, did goodly feats of arms."

"The black was a sign of mourning,'" Launcelot replied; "the green will be of hope, the red—of love."

Dieudonnée went back to her place, her eyes shining. The queen looked at Sir Launcelot inquiringly.

"What mystery is here? Some love matter? Surely not concerning Dieudonnée. It is a jest among my maidens that she scorns love."

Launcelot made no reply. The king, a goodly figure, had ridden into the field and now awaited all comers. Scarcely had he taken his place when a knight in green armor appeared on the east end of the field, and rode forward to meet the king.

The two feutred their spears, and came together as it had been thunder. And the stranger knight with great prowess smote down the king and his horse to the earth. Then the king avoided his horse and threw his shield before him, bidding the stranger alight. The knight obeyed; and the two lashed together strongly, racing and tracing, foining and dashing.

The court was a-tiptoe with excitement.

"They fight like wode men," cried Launcelot. "Now Jesu be praised, this is a noble knight indeed; and if my lord the king be worsted, as it seems indeed he may, I will myself try a fall with the stranger."

The combat grew more furious, neared its climax. At length, the knight in green raised his sword and smote King Arthur such a buffet on his helm that he fell down on his side. Then, waiting for no more, the green knight mounted his horse and galloped off the field so rapidly that none might follow him.

Launcelot rose from his place on the pavilion.

"Send hither my armor, Sir Kaye," he cried. "An this knight return again, I shall be ready to meet him, and avenge my lord the king."

He ran lightly down the pavilion steps, and a little later appeared mounted on the lists, pacing slowly to and fro.

The king left the field, and sent his page to tell the queen his injuries were slight and he would be with her anon. When Arthur came again upon the pavilion he generously rejoiced that Launcelot had consented to joust once more.

"I know well that it is for my sake," he said; "and that he may be rewarded for his pains, Jesu grant that the stranger knight may come back!"

Scarcely had he uttered the words when Guenever touched his arm. Riding across the south side of the field, a knight appeared, clad all in red armor.

"I doubt me not it is the same knight again," said the king, after closely surveying the newcomer. "If he surpass Launcelot—then he hath but to meet Tristram of Cornwall to be champion of the world."

Launcelot and the knight in red rode forward against each other. They met mightily, and what with the strength of the stranger knight's spear. Sir Launcelot's horse fell to the earth, he sitting in the saddle. Then lightly Sir Launcelot avoided his steed, put his shield before him, and drew his sword.

"Alight, thou stranger knight," he cried, "since a mare's son hath so soon failed me! Alight, an thou durst!"

The knight in red dismounted, but did not draw his sword.

"Nay," he said, "I will have no more ado with thee, Launcelot, thou flower of knighthood."

"Thou hast outjousted me on horseback," Launcelot answered. "I beseech thee, fight now with me on foot."

The knight in red shook his head nay.

"I will not so," he replied courteously. "I say I will have no more ado with thee. Thou art wearied with many jousts this day; else could I not have overcome thee."

"I shall quit thee an ever I see my time," said Launcelot. "Beseech thee, then, leave not the field, but come to the king and receive thy reward."

The Tournament at Pentecost was at its height. .   .   .

CHAPTER TWELVE

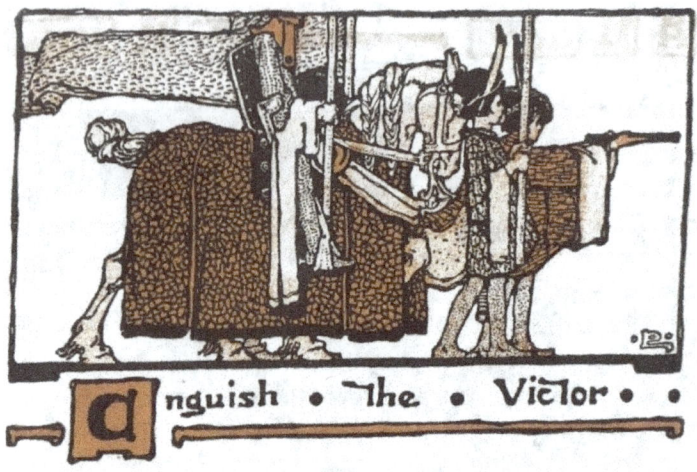

Anguish • The • Victor • •

The court had been watching with interest and curiosity the converse between the knights; and all leaned forward eagerly as the two came towards the pavilion. On reaching it, Launcelot spoke.

"Here is the only knight, my lord king, who within my memory hath e'er outjousted me. He refuses to conclude the combat, and I wait a more fitting opportunity to make clean my record. Prythee, bid him disclose his name and station; and if he be not already of the Table Round, methinks he hath well won a place therein."

"Thy thought is mine," replied the king. "Stranger knight, beseech thee, let us see thy face. An I be not greatly mistaken, thou hast already twice appeared upon the field this day; and each time thou hast proven thyself a valorous man. Bare thy shield, drop thy vizor, and show us to whom belongs the golden circlet, prize of the tournament."

The stranger slowly uncovered his shield, and disclosed one of gold, empty of device or motto. Then he lowered his vizor and looked with sombre, haggard eyes, neither at king nor queen nor court, but straight towards two eyes whose gaze met his as surely as steel and magnet. "Have I atoned?" said his look, and hers answered simply, "Ay."

The king paused a moment in surprise, and a murmur of excited curiosity ran over the court.

"The son of the king of Ireland! Thou art over young, Anguish, for such high deeds as thou hast done this day. Now I bethink me thou art not yet even knight. A twelvemonth since thou didst leave court—"

"And returned but a few days ago with Sir Launcelot," said the queen. As she spoke, she looked sharply at Launcelot, but his face was shadowed by his helmet.

"Ay, it is so," said the king. "Where didst thou find him, Launcelot?"

"In a desert place," answered Launcelot calmly. "We were both bound homeward, so came the rest of the way together."

"Prythee, where hast thou been, Prince Anguish?" the king continued courteously. "Our time now is brief, but we would know where thou hast journeyed; on what high emprise, accomplishing what goodly achievements, to win such prowess as thou hast displayed to-day."

Anguish's gaze left Dieudonnée's, and turned to meet Arthur's.

"My lord the king, you honor me in that you recall so much," he answered; "natheless, that day you gave me leave to travel was not the last time you saw me ere I came home with Sir Launcelot three days since. That morn I asked your leave to go from court I meant not even then to go so soon as I said, nor in that guise. Later I had letters from my sister Isoud—"

"Her beauty and her fame have traveled far," said the king.

"These letters were brought to me," Anguish continued, "by a trusty servant of our house, one Ulfius, a dwarf."

The king and queen started and leaned eagerly forward. The court strained eyes and ears.

"It chanced," said Anguish, "that the dwarf did not reach Camelot with the letters. I met him on his way, and forthwith a whim seized me, mayhap a boy's caprice. It was my fancy to do noble achievements in menial guise, that when I had well won my right to the guerdon of knighthood, I might go to my lady and say, 'Thy poor servant, as a servant, hath done these deeds for thee. In poverty and sorrow have I labored for thy sake. Now crown me knight.' So I dreamed, lord king. We wear the sackcloth and ashes of Lent or ever we share at Easter in the gladness of the risen Jesu."

"'Twas a knightly and Christian thought," the king replied; "and whoever the lady be for whom thou didst thus adventure, she should deem her blest indeed."

Anguish's face had been sad from the time he had dropped his vizor. Now an added shadow fell upon it.

"Say not so," he said, almost sternly. "I went forth in good faith, and with a sturdy heart; but on a false quest was I beguiled. I was Sanslangue, the dumb servant, who came to court with Ulfius that day a twelvemonth since. He had been a slave among the Saracens, and knew much of the Black Art; so upon all your eyes he cast a spell so that ye knew me not. Merlin was not befooled—nor one other. And so I went forth—ah, lord king, question me no further now here before all men! This year past, I have done no noble deeds, but have lain in lecherous ease in the arms of a sorceress."

King and court were absolutely silent for a surprised second. Launcelot made a step forward, and opened his lips as if to speak. Anguish stayed him with a gesture.

"To-day," he said, rapidly and bitterly, "to-day I have jousted to win back my honor which I have so much besmeared. I could not have succeeded after my year's slothful shame save for one thing—the desire to kneel at my lady's feet and say, 'Take this for atonement, for earnest of my future deeds.' May it be?"

Across the space that divided them, he asked the question of Dieudonnée; but she alone made no audible reply. A mighty shout of applause and assent went up from all the company. But Dieudonnée sat with her face hidden in her hands.

"Thou hast thy answer. Prince Anguish," said Arthur, after the tumult had subsided. "To-morrow I shall dub thee knight. Give him now, Guenever, the golden circlet, and let him crown his lady if she be of the court."

Guenever placed the golden circlet on the point of Anguish's spear, which he lowered for that purpose. An instant later he held the victor's token in his hand.

"One moment, my lord king," he said. "Ulfius my servant spoke for me when he asked of you three boons last Pentecost. One you gave him, and me through him. May I now claim the other two?"

"Thou mayst, assuredly, fair son," said Arthur.

"One you have promised me without the asking," Anguish said. "That is knighthood. The other—"

He paused, and leaped lightly from his horse. He passed through the crowd about the pavilion, and mounted its steps, all men's eyes fixed upon him. He reached at length Dieudonnée, still sitting with her face covered.

"Dieudonnée," he said, "wilt be crowned my lady now?"

She dropped her trembling hands and looked up at him with eyes which for the first time he saw answer the love in his.

"My lord!" she breathed. He laid upon her loosely flowing golden hair the circlet, victor's trophy of the jousts; then took her by the hand. She rose, and together they went and stood before the king and queen.

"The third boon I crave now, King Arthur," Anguish said; "that having been knighted I may be wed to-morrow mom."

Dieudonnée gave a quick start.

"Would that I could grant all boons so gladly," Arthur answered. "The Archbishop that wedded me shall perform the ceremony; and Jesu and His Mother Mary send blessings on you both!"

Anguish felt Dieudonnée trembling within the circle of his arm.

"It is well," he said. "I thank you, my lord king." Then to Dieudonnée he turned and spoke low, "Godgiven, God-given, to-morrow mine, forever mine!"

She made no answer, trembling still.

CHAPTER THIRTEEN

The · Wedding · Morn · of · Anguish

In the pale dawn of the next morning, Dieudonnée arose; and having robed with rapid fingers, slipped noiselessly from her sleeping-chamber, and along the silent hallways. Reaching at length the chapel, she hesitated an instant on the threshold, her hand pressed upon her heart. Then she pushed open the door, and entered.

Two esquires knelt just within, and a priest bowed before the altar, where was displayed the naked Host. A drawn sword and Anguish's golden shield lay beneath it, and beside the chancel rail, his eyes fixed upon God's Body, his hands clasped in prayer, knelt Anguish in still adoration. Dieudonnee looked at the two esquires in mute inquiry. They bowed, and she passed noiselessly up the aisle, and touched Anguish on the shoulder.

He started and turned. His face, white and spiritualized by fasting and meditation, smiled at her. She stood, slender and pale in the ghostly light of the early day, looking down at him. Her white face and white garments suggested a burial rather than a bridal. Her eyes spoke woe that rent his heart, and she seemed the despairing ghost of a happiness long dead.

"Hast thou yet shrived thee?" she whispered.

He shook his head.

"I must speak with thee before thou dost," she said imperatively, "at once. Last night I had no opportunity. Deny me not."

He rose immediately. The priest turned from the altar, and looked surprise and displeasure as he saw Dieudonnée.

"The day has dawned, the vigil is over," Anguish said to him in a low voice. "Prythee, leave us, father. We would speak together for a little space."

"It is not fitting," answered the priest. "E'en she who is to be thy wife has no place here. Thy thoughts should be alone of heaven now."

"They are of heaven when she is here," said Anguish. "Fear not, father. I will shrive me anon."

The priest shook his head, but left the altar, first replacing the Host in the pyx. The two esquires, seeing his departure, likewise left the chapel, and Anguish and Dieudonnée were alone. He looked at her questioningly. Both her hands were clasped upon her heart. The pale light of dawn encircled her. She turned her eyes to the crucifix on the altar, and for an instant they reflected the torture in the sculptured Face.

"Farewell, my happiness," she said; then looked again at Anguish.

"I have that to say to thee which must be said speedily," she said. "Remember first what I told thee that evening in the rose-bower, when thou didst speak of thy love; that thou didst know me not."

He gazed at her, perplexed, but made no reply.

"Then," she went on in a measured voice, "then I did not love thee. Now—" she caught herself abruptly. "Shortly thou wilt be shrived and houselled, and then made knight; but first, ere thou art confessed, I must shrive me. So as a penitent, I kneel to thee, having wronged thee much."

She sank upon her knees. He would have stayed her with a protest; but she prevented him. He bent over her.

"Turn thy face away," she said, her voice a prayer. "So. Now I will tell thee."

She whispered a sentence in his ear.

He stood as if turned to stone. She waited passively, her hands still clasped. He leaned down and caught them in his, almost roughly.

"No, no," he said, his voice hoarse, beseeching, broken. "No, no. Thou art wode—thou art dreaming—"

"Nay," she said only, in a tone blank either of pain or entreaty.

He stared at her, his eyes large, his face white. She knelt still, pale, determined, inscrutable. He uttered at length an exclamation of horror. A smile sadder than tears touched her lips at the sound.

"God's wounds!" he muttered in a thick voice. "God's wounds! Are all things dreams alike?"

Presently, he seized his sword from its place before the altar, and made as if to pierce her heart.

"Take thy guerdon," he said brutally.

"With joy," she said.

Her readiness disarmed him, and also perchance the thought of the deed so nearly done. He dropped the weapon with a crash, turned from her, and clung for support to a pillar nearby. Heavy, tearless sobs tore his breast, and echoed in the dawn. Dieudonnée watched him, and had he looked at her then, he would have seen all her heart in her eyes. She made no movement, said no word.

Slowly he mastered his emotion, but did not stir. At last she rose.

"It is farewell, then, Anguish," she said quietly.

He moved slowly, and as he turned, a blue scarf fluttered an instant at his bosom, then lay beside his sword on the floor. She walked towards the chapel door. As she reached it. Anguish spoke.

"Whither goest thou?" he said.

"I know not," she answered, and therein spoke sooth.

At a sign from him she drew near again. The first ray of the sun flashed suddenly through a high window above their heads, and a bird's sweet song broke the stillness. When it had ceased, he said hoarsely:

"The court looks for us to wed this morn—I would not blot thy name.—Last night I received letters from my sister Isoud, calling me imperatively to my father's court. I had meant to take thee with me. Now—"

A sob seemed to choke him, but he forced it back.

"Meseems we must perforce go through the wedding Mass," he said. "I could leave thee then at once—and later—"

He paused. She bent her head, struggling with her tears as she saw him evade her look.

"As thou wilt, my lord," she said. "I shall not be here when thou dost return."

Her hands, clasped until now, fell by her side, and with the movement there dropped from them upon the blue samite scarf a withered rose. She turned again to leave the chapel. As she opened the door, she looked back at the altar. Before it lay the fallen sword, the blue scarf, the faded rose. She gazed at them whitely a moment, wondering dully where she had seen them before. Then suddenly she remembered. Merlin's vision had come true—ah, Jesu, yes! She gave a sudden choking breath.

"It is the grave of love," she said; "of his love."

The door closed behind her.

Anguish fell upon the steps of the altar.

CHAPTER FOURTEEN

The • Bride • Unwived •

The wedding Mass had nearly reached its close. The Archbishop had turned to dismiss the people, when there was a sudden tumult in the hallway, and a messenger entered the chapel hastily. He was covered with mud, and seemed to have ridden far. He rushed up to the bridegroom kneeling before the altar.

"Letters, my lord, from thy sister Isoud," he said.

"Soothly," said King Arthur, rising from his place in displeasure, "soothly, thy summons must be urgent, that thou dost enter with so scant ceremony this holy place at this holy time."

"*They are, indeed. King Arthur," answered the messenger. "My lord the prince will tell you so when he has read the letters."

Anguish perused them hastily. Then he went and knelt before the king.

"Prythee, my lord king, pardon this haste, this unseemly interruption. My sister Isoud calls me to her side, and I must go at once."

"And leave thy new-made bride?" asked the king in strong surprise. "Methinks a wife's place is higher than a sister's."

"Thou speakest sooth," answered Anguish; "but it may be a matter of life and death if I go not. I will leave my bride in the queen's keeping—"

Guenever uttered an exclamation.

"Surely she goes with thee?"

"The journey is over long and rough for a woman," Anguish replied, "and Isoud's call is urgent."

"What say'st thou, Lady Dieudonnée?" asked the king.

"It is as my lord wills," answered Dieudonnée quietly.

"Well, we will guard her for thee, Anguish," said the king. "It is a perverse fate indeed that it so chances. Stay not upon the order of thy going, but go at once. Speak the blessing, your Grace, and then to horse, Prince Anguish."

"Queen Isoud sent letters also to Queen Guenever," said the messenger. He gave them to the queen, who, with an exclamation of pleasure, opened and perused them rapidly.

"Ah, these I must answer," she cried. "Thou wilt wait long enough for that, Prince Anguish?"

"Ay, my queen," he answered. "I beseech thee, however, make haste."

The Archbishop uttered the long-deferred *Ite missa est,* and the court streamed out of the chapel. Anguish went to order his horse, and Guenever bade Dieudonnée follow to the queen's chamber. When they had entered it, Guenever turned upon the bride.

"Wilt thou let him go alone?" she asked.

"It is a woman's part to obey," Dieudonnée answered in an even voice.

The queen pouted.

"It is not best for lovers to part," she said positively. "Might it not—it came to me at the end of the Mass—" She paused, pulled Dieudonnée towards her and whispered in her ear. Dieudonnée's eyes grew larger as she listened, her hands crept upward involuntarily and clasped themselves above her heart. When Guenever had finished, she did not speak at once. Then she said, looking at the queen:

"Why?"

"Why?" repeated Guenever, in a puzzled tone.

"Ay," said Dieudonnée in a voice low and controlled. "Why? Thou hast no love for me."

Guenever broke forth into protestations. In the midst of them, Dieudonnée smiled.

"Ah, I know now," she said. "Thou dost wish to rid thyself of me. Well, so be it—if thus I may serve my lord. He will not otherwise. Write the letters, and I will prepare myself."

She left Guenever, and once out of sight, flew down the hall like a mad thing. Reaching at length her room, she changed her dress rapidly; then once more sped along the corridors, and left the castle. She succeeded in reaching the forest unobserved, and hastened through it until at last she stood beneath Merlin's oak.

Merlin, who had been at neither the knighting nor the wedding ceremonies, sat in his usual place, quiet, inscrutable. As he saw her he spoke.

"So thou hast come again. Thou hast not been here since—"

"Nay, nay," said Dieudonnée, her voice shaking, her words indistinct. "Nay, not since that day I swooned here at thy feet. I did not come to thee fearing then, Merlin, but since I have feared thee. But not so now. I have come to ask thee as some women ask a priest—but priests are not for me—"

She paused, a piteous figure, shaken quite out of her usual self-control. Anon she would return again to her sternly-ruled habit of composure, but now she stood there undisguised, woeful, despairing. Merlin sighed.

"Why hast thou come to me now?" he said.

"To know," answered Dieudonnée pantingly, "to know one thing. The queen has just proposed—"

"I know," said Merlin quietly.

"Jesu be thanked!" said Dieudonnée. "Is it best then that I should do this thing, or shall I, as was my first thought, end all now? Tell me, Merlin, if thou canst, of charity."

"What deemest thou best?" asked Merlin quietly.

"What deem I best?" repeated Dieudonnée passionately. "To serve my lord, an it were but humbly—to love him eternally—to die for him, body and soul."

"Go," said Merlin.

"It is enough," said Dieudonnée. A great look of joy swept away the shadows in her sombre eyes.

"Seekest thou nothing for thyself?" said Merlin gently.

Dieudonnée made a gesture as if casting some slight thing away.

"Nay," she answered quietly. "I thank thee, Merlin. Farewell. If thou dost never see me more, remember my life was of little worth to me, my love very great. If I lose the one to serve the other, I shall be well content."

She left him as rapidly as she had come. Merlin sat motionless, watching her until the last glimpse of her dress had disappeared among the trees. Then he sighed and stirred.

"Ah, God!" he said aloud. "This love, when love it is—whence comes it, and what means it, God?"

CHAPTER FIFTEEN

L a · Beale · Isoud

Isoud of Ireland stood in the doorway of her father's castle, her red-gold hair blown in the wind. It was late June, and a cool morning. The young queen, shading her eyes with her hand, looked anxiously across the open country, and frowned with impatience.

"Laggard!" she cried petulantly. "An he come not anon, he need not come at all. My business needeth haste. Bragwaine," she turned to her handmaid standing behind her, "Bragwaine, thou art positive the messenger was swift and sure?"

"Ay, madam," Bragwaine answered.

"There is naught to do but wait then," said Isoud, sighing. "Ah, Jesu! how ill I like that! Let us within, Bragwaine. It grows chill."

"Stay, madam," said her serving-woman. "Look, yonder is a cloud of dust."

Isoud obeyed eagerly.

"Ay," she cried, clapping her hands, "ay, it is. Oh, if this be Anguish, two votive candles to the Blessed Mother, whom I have besieged with prayers—"

She ran down the steps impulsively. Not satisfied with this, she sped across the courtyard, and stood at length straining her great gray eyes towards the cloud of dust, gradually resolving itself into shape.

"Is it verily Anguish? Ah, sweet Mother! If instead it were Mark my husband, Bragwaine! If Anguish come not to-day—Ah, it is, it is! See, he rides alone save for an esquire and—oh, Jesu! is he minded to go on a pilgrimage? Behold a monk rides also with him. Methinks the holy man will scarce approve of me." She laughed, almost dancing with impatience.

"Ah, he is slow, but his horse is weary. Good brother! I knew he would come at my call. There! now thou canst behold his black curls, Bragwaine. They say we have eyes alike. Once I asked Tristram—At last he sees me."

She seized her rose-colored scarf, and let it flutter on the breeze.

"Welcome, dear brother, welcome," she cried, her burnished hair bright in the sun. 'Take this for greeting, and anon my lips. Would not Tristram love him well, Bragwaine?"

An instant later. Anguish and his two attendants rode across the drawbridge. Isoud ran impulsively halfway, and threw herself against her brother, mounted on his horse, at imminent danger of unseating him. The horse reared and plunged. Anguish, with an exclamation, caught Isoud about the waist and swung her lightly into the saddle. She clung to him in silence for a moment, while he quieted the horse. Then with a bright smile she turned her face upward to his.

"Ah, good Anguish, I knew thou wouldst not fail me! Kiss me, and let me thank thee."

Anguish obeyed somewhat absently.

"Wilt dismount now, Isoud?" he said- methinks the horse is quiet."

"Nay," said Isoud positively, nestling closer to him. "Nay, I will not dismount. Let us ride thus to the castle together. When we were children, we used often—"

"Bethink thee," said Anguish gravely. "Thou art queen of Cornwall and princess of Ireland. Is it fitting that—"

Isoud covered his mouth with her white hand.

"Thou hast indeed learned propriety in Arthur's court," she cried, laughing. "Is it thus that Sir Launcelot speaks to Queen Guenever? Nay," she settled herself somewhat more comfortably. "Because I am queen of Cornwall and princess of Ireland, I will e'en do as I please. Go on."

Anguish complied without more protest. The two rode on together, Isoud's golden hair beside his black curls bared of the helmet. The monk and the esquire rode behind. As they went, Isoud said, glancing at her brother's attendants:

"Who is thy esquire? And Ulfius is not with thee. Where is Ulfius?"

A shadow of pain fell on Anguish's face.

"Ah, Isoud, I have much to tell thee," he replied. "Ask not for Ulfius. He is dead; and he died serving me."

"Then he died a happy death," answered Isoud dauntlessly. "For the faithful, it is good to die for one beloved; and Ulfius loved thee well. Tell me more when thou desirest, Anguish. Who is thy esquire, then?"

"One Ector hight, of Arthur's court," replied Anguish indifferently. "He was given to me by Sir Launcelot, and for the monk—"

Isoud laughed, and shook her finger at him.

"Ay, why dost thou travel with a monk?"

"'Twas at Queen Guenever's request,'* Anguish answered. "She desired to send letters and messages to thee, and protested that they must be borne by holy hands. He has traveled well, and given us ghostly succor. The queen commended him to my good graces, and to thine."

"I will receive him anon," said Isoud. "Ah, it is time to dismount; so once more, welcome, dear brother, welcome home."

She turned and kissed him again impulsively; then dropped lightly to the ground. Bragwaine joined her, and the two women went up the steps together.

"When thou hast rested and refreshed thee," Isoud called back to Anguish, "come to me. I would talk with thee o'er many things."

An hour later Anguish joined her.

Isoud was alone, and as Anguish entered, she sprang up to greet him.

"Come, sit beside me at the lattice," she cried, "and first tell me all, all that has chanced to thee since my father left thee at Arthur's court."

"That," answered Anguish, after an instant's pause, "that, Isoud, is a somewhat long story. Were it not better, since it seems the case is urgent, that thou shouldst first tell me why thou didst call me hither?"

Isoud's face flushed into earnestness. She looked up at him, her hands clasped.

"Ay, perhaps. Then listen, Anguish. I sent for thee that ere my husband Mark comes hither to take me back to Cornwall, I may go in thy care to Sir Launcelot's castle, Joyous Garde."

Anguish looked perplexed. "Wherefore?" he said.

Isoud frowned. "Has the news not traveled to Arthur's court?" she said. "King Mark, my husband, hath put my Lord Tristram in prison."

Anguish started in dismay.

"Nay," he said; "the flower of knighthood, save only Sir Launcelot,—how came he in such evil pass?"

Isoud set her lips.

"Mark suspected," she answered curtly. "Thou knowst his nature. And when he did this foul deed, I was so sore angered that I came forthwith to visit my father of Ireland."

She looked at Anguish roguishly. Her brother's face relaxed into a laugh.

"So," she went on, "my Lord Tristram sent me a letter, praying me to be his good lady; and if it pleased me to make ready a vessel for him and me, he would go with me into Arthur's realm. Whenas, I sent back word to be of good comfort, for I would make the vessel ready—"

She paused and looked at Anguish beseechingly.

"And thou, dear brother, must take me to meet my Lord Tristram, and thus accompany us to Joyous Garde, whither Sir Launcelot has bid us come whenever we would. Later we shall visit Arthur's court, and I shall see Queen Guenever, and Tristram will joust with Launcelot, as both have long desired."

"That me reminds," said Anguish, "that in the outer chamber the monk waits with letters for thee from Queen Guenever. Wilt receive him now?"

"Anon," said Isoud; "but first, what sayest thou to my request, dear brother?"

"King Mark?" said Anguish somewhat doubtfully.

"Oh, he!" Isoud snapped her fingers lightly. "I sent word to Sir Dinas and Sir Sadok to take King Mark and keep him in prison until I had departed to meet my Lord Tristram. I had fear that he might escape before thou didst reach me. Now—" she threw out her hands in conclusion.

"Ah, Isoud," said Anguish, looking at her wistfully, "ah, Isoud, thou art blessed indeed among ladies. Thou knowst what love is."

"Thou speakest sadly," said Isoud. "Dost not also know love, dear brother? Methinks thou art over grave and sad. Hath some fair lady scorned thee?"

Anguish evaded the question.

"The tale is long," he answered. "Anon. Now wilt thou see the monk, Isoud—An it so please thee, we will start to-morrow morn for Joyous Garde."

"I thank thee," said Isoud. "Go now, and send the monk."

A few minutes later, the monk appeared. He stood impassively, his hands clasped together under his long flowing sleeves, his eyes downcast. Isoud greeted him courteously and bade him be seated. Then she said:

"Now what news hast thou for me? And by what name am I to call thee, brother?"

"In religion, fair daughter, my name is Brother Trestriste," answered the monk, "and I have letters and messages for thee from Queen Guenever."

As the monk handed them to her, Isoud noticed idly that his hands were white and slender. The next instant, she was absorbed in the letters.

Unseen, the monk lifted his bent head, and gazed at her. In his face there was both anxiety and appeal, a kind of strained intensity in the whole figure. Presently Isoud, concluding the letters, stirred and laughed, and at the sound the monk again bent his head, and stood with clasped hands.

The young queen rose.

"So. It is a good letter thou hast brought me, brother. And now what message? Queen Guenever tells me here that thou hast something else of importance to say to me which she could not well write, and commends thee to my good graces. Speak freely then, good brother."

The monk hesitated an instant. Isoud noted that his hair was jet-black, making whiter by contrast the pale skin. The eyes, large, of a blue almost black, gazed half fearfully, half appealingly into hers. The next instant he was at her feet, weeping. Isoud, distressed and somewhat scandalized, strove to raise him, but he resisted.

"Madam," he said at length brokenly, "madam, Queen Isoud, promise me to keep secret what I shall tell thee now. Only Queen Guenever knows."

Isoud promised instantly. The monk, crouching at her feet, sat upright, and fixed his eyes, somewhat desperate now, upon her face.

"Madam," he said, "I am no monk, but a woman."

Isoud gave a startled exclamation. Brother Trestriste lifted his hand in warning.

"Hist, madam, beseech thee. I am a woman of Cameliard, Queen Guenever's birthplace, and the day we left Camelot, I was wedded to thy brother Anguish."

"Anguish!" repeated Isoud in a stupefied tone. "Anguish!" She looked at the kneeling figure with a quick suspicion. "And he knows not who thou art? How chances it thou dost not travel according to thy station as wife of the Prince of Ireland? And what dost thou in the guise of a monk?"

"I will tell thee all," answered Dieudonnée in a low voice. Now that her chief revelation was made, her agitation was stilled, and she spoke more calmly. "I am here, madam, in this guise, because I love. As thou lovest, do thou listen to me and be merciful."

Isoud looked at her, suspicion still lingering. Then her face cleared, and her eyes grew tender.

"Ah, poor soul, blessed soul," she said, "since thou art a lover, I will indeed thee love. Not there thy place at my feet, but here beside me." She seated herself at the window, and held out her hands. "Come hither, and fear not. I am also a servant of Love."

Dieudonnée looked at her unbelievingly. Isoud gazed back with dauntless pity. Dieudonnée rose, her white monkish garments falling straitly about her, and made a step towards the young queen. The next moment the two were in each other's arms.

"See now, we love each other already!" cried Isoud. "How art thou hight, my sister."

Dieudonnée breathed her name.

"Dieudonnee," repeated Isoud, her voice lingering on the word. "Now tell me all, Dieudonnée."

The two were closeted together for an hour. When Dieudonnée had at last finished, Isoud sat in silence for a space, her eyes dreamy.

"And he has never known thee?" she said at length.

"Never," answered Dieudonnée.

"One thing only troubles me," said Isoud softly; "is not this garb of thine a sin against Holy Church?"

Dieudonnée laughed, somewhat bitterly.

"I have sinned much against the Church ere this, the priests say," she said, looking up at Isoud rather recklessly. "And now, if I add to it, the sin is mine." She shrugged her shoulders slightly.

"It is for love," said Isoud determinedly, as if trying to convince herself. "God will forgive thee, Dieudonnée. And so will Anguish when he knows the truth."

Dieudonnée shivered.

"I know not," she answered, looking at Isoud with wide, mournful eyes; "but this I know, Isoud. If I live, I must be with my lord, and there is no other way. With esquire he was already provided, else might I have followed him as page."

Isoud kissed her.

"All will be well," she said. "And when Anguish leaves me—let time decide. Meantime—Anguish's wife, my sister—ah, I am glad that thou art come to me, Dieudonnée!"

CHAPTER SIXTEEN

Anguish's • Vision

At Joyous Garde, Mass was being celebrated; and Anguish, kneeling devoutly, strove to attend strictly to the duties proper to the place and time. He found it somewhat difficult to do so. In the place of honor, where Launcelot was wont to sit when he was at home, Isoud knelt, her red-gold hair shining through its cover of silver tissue. Beside her was young Tristram of Cornwall, Isoud's lover, and flower of knighthood, saving always Sir Launcelot. These two, whom Fate had brought irrevocably together, were now in their rightful places. King Mark of Cornwall might rage in prison, and Isoud of the White Hands languish in Brittany; Tristram, hunter, knight, minstrel, lover, Isoud, rose of the world, were side by side. It was enough.

A priest, stout and rubicund, was upon the altar, cheerfully singing the Mass, and speedily, as befitted one who knew that my Lord Tristram waited to go a-hunting. The monk, Brother Trestriste, acting as Server, moved lightly from place to place, and did his devoirs with rapid grace. Anguish's eyes, resting idly upon him now and then, noticed that his hands were white and beautiful. Where had he seen such hands before? He puzzled vainly for an instant; then recollected; and at the memory frowned and bit his lips. Where was she now, false-hearted, who had spoiled his life? Surely, Fate had used him ill, to bring into his life first a Hellayne and then a Dieudonnée. He pitied himself sorely.

The first bell rang for the Elevation, and Anguish, shocked into pious recollection, bowed with the others, and beat his breast. Nevertheless, his thoughts wandered. Now he remembered her dislike of priests, and he had not seen her often at the sacring of the Mass. Maids should be devout and holy, and love well the sacred Mysteries of the Church.

The bell rang again, and Anguish, bowing low, with a mighty effort cast the thought of Dieudonnée from his mind. Instead of such worldly matters and unholy, rather would he beseech God, now present in the Bread, to show him what to do with his marred and broken life. He had fulfilled his sister's desire, and brought her to Tristram. Now for Anguish of Ireland, what?

The bell rang a third time, and Anguish prayed—

"Fair sweet Jesu, whose man I am, and servant day and night, show me, I beseech Thee, how to use what remains to me of years. Thou knowest, O Blessed Lord, that I am over young to have tasted so great sin and sorrow; but since my life is blighted, show me Thy pleasure as to how I am to serve Thee. In the Name of the Father, and of the Son, and of the Holy Ghost. Amen."

He waited in the breathless hush of the Elevation, and, bold in his desire and in his prayer, dared to lift his eyes for an instant to the bared Host, shining in its bejeweled pyx. A single ray of light beamed suddenly upon it, and its radiance seemed to come directly towards himself; a ray of light, blood-red, staining in its course the white garments of Brother Trestriste. Anguish beheld it, awed, wondering.

"It is a sign," he said to himself.

The Mass went on with rapidity. The minutes passed, and the hunting-party waited. The good father was considerate. At length the priest dismissed the congregation with his blessing, and the assemblage streamed out of the chapel in haste. Anguish alone remained kneeling; and Isoud paused beside him in surprise.

"Anguish! Dost not go on the hunt with my Lord Tristram? He will much wonder—"

"Nay," replied Anguish. "I have other business of import, sister. I pray thee, make my excuses to Sir Tristram. I will not hunt to-day."

Isoud passed on, and in a few moments the chapel was empty. The stout priest who had celebrated Mass had hurried away to join the hunt, leaving his Server to remove the holy vessels. Anguish watched him in silence for a space. Finally, as Brother Trestriste turned to leave the altar, Anguish rose and went to the chancel rail.

"I would speak with thee a moment, brother, on a matter of ghostly import," he said.

The monk started; then he recovered himself, and looked at Anguish gravely.

"Were it not best to consult Father Anthony?" he said.

Anguish impatiently waved aside the proposition.

"Nay," he said; "Father Anthony is scarce to my liking in this matter. It is not a question of confession, but of advice. Prythee, do not deny me."

The monk hesitated, then yielded. He left the altar, and came down to Anguish.

"I am ready," he said.

Anguish fell on his knees, and crossed himself.

"Just now at Mass," he began, "methought I saw a vision, and I come to thee to learn its import, I prayed the most sweet Jesu that He would show me what next to do in this my life, so perplexed and crossed; and I saw—"

His voice sank to a reverent whisper as he described what he deemed a sign from heaven. When he had finished, he looked at Brother Trestriste anxiously.

The monk hesitated a moment.

"What did thy heart tell thee was its meaning?" he said gently at last.

"Brother," replied Anguish, "methought, perchance, that ray of blood-red light shining on the sacred Host, and staining in its course thy garments of purity, was a sign from heaven sent to bid me go in quest of the Sangreal. Many brave knights, thou knowest, have gone from Arthur's court on the holy journey. Once I dreamed also of that high quest; but since then I have sinned; and 'tis said that only the sinless can achieve the Vision—"

He paused. The monk was silent.

"Natheless, even if I fail," said Anguish, "methinks I shall die on a holy quest; and see in death, perchance, what my living eyes through sinfulness may not behold. What thinkst thou, brother? Is my worthiness sufficient to go forth on this holy journey?"

"Soothly ay," the monk answered, with singular passion. "Thou hast sinned. So did many of the great saints of the Church. Life hath dealt hardly with thee. Our Lord Himself walked thorny paths. This thought of thine, meseems, is a high and holy one, doubtless sent from heaven. Do not lightly spurn it. The repentant, perchance, as well as the sinless, may achieve the holy Vision of the Sangreal."

"Thy words fit with my thought," said Anguish. "I will then go upon this quest. Now bless me, brother; and to-morrow I shall be shrived and receive my Saviour, and so hie forth as holily as may be."

He bent his head. The monk lifted trembling hands in benediction. Then Anguish rose.

"I will go with thee," said Brother Trestriste, rapidly and somewhat pleadingly, "Thou mayst need me." Anguish looked doubtful.

"I know not whither my quest will lead me," he said. "Natheless it would be well to have ghostly counsel at need. On such a journey the presence of a monk surely might aid me much."

He knelt again before the altar. Brother Trestriste left the chapel with quiet steps. Anguish would have been much amazed had he seen the monk as he reached privacy. Brother Trestriste fell upon his knees, sobbing bitterly.

"He knew me not," he said wildly and unreasonably; "he knew me not."

nguish alone remained o o
o o o o kneeling

At · The · Castle · of · Carbonek ·

Brother Trestriste clung to Queen Isoud in silence.

"Ah," said the latter at length, releasing him with a sigh; "it is well for thee to go, and I wish thee all joy, dear Dieudonnée." She paused and laughed a little. "Perchance for the sake of my good name, 'tis well that thou departest; else might King Mark have another scandal toward me."

Dieudonnée smiled.

"I also am loth to part with thee," she said, looking at Isoud tenderly. "If ever I may come to thee indeed in my own person—"

"If!" cried Isoud with a kiss. "If me no ifs! Anguish is a blind bat, and so I expect to tell him some time. Till that happy hour, Godspeed, my sister Dieudonnée."

The two kissed again, and parted. Isoud followed Brother Trestriste, and took leave of Anguish at the doorway. Tristram had not yet returned from the hunt of the day before.

"Farewell, my brother," said Isoud, as Anguish bent to kiss her; "God give thee love, say I, God give thee love!"

Anguish frowned slightly.

"Prythee, change thy words, Isoud," he said, "'Tis not on a love-quest that I am bound."

"Nay, I will not change," said Isoud wilfully. "God gives us nothing better; so again, God give thee—what thou most desirest."

She wafted him a kiss from her slender fingertips. Anguish and the monk rode from the castle-door together. Isoud stood watching them long. When at last she turned, there were tears in her eyes.

"Alas!" she said. "My heart misgives me I shall never see them more."

The knight and the monk rode slowly in silence for a space.

"Brother," said Anguish at length, "I shall in this adventure be guided largely by your advice, since methinks in the matter of the Sangreal, monk is better judge than knight. Rumor hath it that at the Castle of Carbonek, the Holy Cup is preserved. Shall we there first?"

"It likes me well," Brother Trestriste replied.

At evening the next day, Anguish and the monk entered Carbonek Castle, and were made welcome by King Pelles, its master. They reached the castle just in time for the evening repast, and Anguish was given a seat near King Pelles and his daughter, the fair Elaine, mother of Galahad.

While they talked at meat, of a sudden a great silence fell upon all the hall. And Anguish, turning with the rest towards the window, beheld a snow-white dove flying therein, and in her mouth a little censer of gold. Then was he aware of a sweet savor filling the hall as if the incense from all the Masses in the world had been collected on the instant in that little space. Anguish, turning in awe and wonder towards the table, beheld thereon all manner of meats and drinks, such as had not been there before the coming of the dove.

Then, ere he had time to cease marveling at this, a damosel entered the hall, passing fair and young, and bearing a vessel of gold betwixt her palms. Therewith with one accord, the whole table bent the knee, and with King Pelles, devoutly recited their prayers. The damosel passed from the hall, and the miracle ended, all arose. Anguish looked towards King Pelles.

"Ah, sweet Jesu!" he said. "What is this?"

"That which thou seekest, fair son," King Pelles answered reverently; "the richest thing that any man hath living; the holy Sangreal."

Anguish crossed himself.

"And may no man further attain it?" he said.

The king looked reflective.

"When this thing goeth about," he said at last, "the Round Table shall be broken. Here shall no knight win worship, but if he be of worship himself, and good living, and loveth God, and dreadeth God; else he gaineth no worship here, be he never so hardy."

Anguish's head sank humbly on his breast.

"I know not whether I be worthy," he said, "but it is to know that I came. Wherefore, King Pelles, by your leave, I will lie in the castle this night."

"Ye shall not do so by my counsel," the king answered, "for it is hard and ye escape without shame."

"I shall take the adventure that shall befall me," said Anguish, shutting close his lips.

"Be shriven clean then, and make you ready," said King Pelles, "and ye shall see what shall chance."

That night, having him confessed, Anguish was led to a fair large chamber, and around it were many shut doors. He lay down in his armor and waited. He was long awake, but at last wearied from his journey, he fell asleep. Suddenly he was aroused by a bright light streaming across the bed, and in its radiance he saw a great spear coming straight towards him. Ere he was aware, the spear-head smote him on the shoulder and wounded him sorely. Scarcely had this chanced when a knight appeared, fully armed, and bade Anguish arise to fight him.

Anguish obeyed. He dressed his shield, and there began a mighty combat. The blood fell fast.

They gave each other many sore strokes. At length Anguish smote the stranger knight so mightily on the helm that he fell upon his knees. Ere Anguish could ask his name, however, he disappeared.

Once more Anguish laid him down to rest, but peace was not long allowed him. Of a sudden there were shots of darts and arrows falling thick and fast upon him, and hurting him sore. Then came many animals into the room, a lion, a dragon, and a leopard, and with each in turn Anguish did combat and was victor. At last entered an old man, who seated himself on a chair, and, playing a harp, sang an old song of Joseph of Armathie, guardian of the Holy Grail. And when he had finished, he turned and spoke to Anguish.

"Thou hast done well," he said. "Go now from hence. Ye have done well, and better shall ye do hereafter; but here ye shall have no more adventures."

And with that he vanished, and forthwith there came through the window the white dove with the golden censer, and the chamber Anguish lay in was filled with sweet savors. Then as in a vision he beheld four children bearing four tapers, and in their midst walked an old man with a censer in one hand and a spear in the other. Following him came four damsels, clad in pure white; and Anguish saw them enter as it were a great chamber filled with light. They kneeled before an altar of silver, and another, in a bishop's dress, kneeled likewise before it. Above the head of the holy man there hovered a shining sword, so piercing in its brightness that for a moment Anguish was blinded. As he closed his eyes he heard a voice.

"Go hence, Sir Anguish," it said. "As yet thou art not worthy for to be in this place." And with that he fell into a deep sleep, from which he did not waken until mom.

As he came out of the chamber at daybreak, he met Brother Trestriste at the door. The monk was very pale.

"Didst sleep well. Sir Anguish?" he asked.

Anguish smiled.

"Soothly I scarce know," he answered; and to the monk it seemed that there was a new softness in both face and voice. "I have seen visions this night, and heard many marvels. What they are, what they mean, I cannot tell; but this I know, I will no further rest me by my will until I have achieved the Sangreal."

CHAPTER EIGHTEEN

In · the · Forest ·

Anguish and the monk rode through the forest together.

"Now counsel me, brother," said Anguish, "he shall have much earthly worship that shall bring to an end the quest of the Sangreal."

"I talked with the priest at Castle Carbonek," Brother Trestriste replied. "Methought that he, dwelling on the spot where such marvels chanced, could give us good counsel. He said little save that which thou knowest already."

"Tell me, natheless," said Anguish eagerly.

"None shall attain the Vision, saith he," answered the monk, his dreamy eyes fixed on the green tangle of the forest stretching beyond—"none save by cleanness or pure confession. Also he bade

me tell thee to eat none other save bread and water
till thou shouldst achieve the Sangreal."

Anguish crossed himself.

"I will do so," he said devoutly. "I thank thee,
brother. I must search me now where I may have
the Sacrament. No hermitage must I pass, nor holy
house, without therein receiving my Lord."

"It is well resolved," replied the monk somewhat
listlessly. Anguish fell a-musing, and the two rode
on together for a space in silence.

"Son," said the monk at length abruptly; "son,
tell me why thou art of a sudden bound upon this
quest. Thou wilt answer, perchance, because thou
wert vouchsafed a vision at Joyous Garde. But ere
that time—what was it that made life a bitter thing
to thee?"

"Brother," said Anguish, "it is true that my life
hath grown of little worth to me; so I have devoted
the poor remnant to God's service."

"Methinks, if that be true, God gives thee little
thanks," the monk replied. "Why didst not offer to
Him thy life when it was precious to thee?"

"Prythee recall not to me that bitter time," said
Anguish sharply. "In brief, brother, I loved a
woman, and for her sake I would have given all my
life."

"Can love ever die?" said the monk, as if to
himself.

"Once I thought not," said Anguish; "but,
brother, she was not worthy."

The monk was silent. He was riding a few paces
behind Anguish, and at the words he stretched out

his arms impulsively to the young knight riding in front of him. An instant only; then he recollected himself, and spoke calmly.

"Thou didst, of course, fair son, offer to thy newmade wife all that man should give?"

Anguish winced. The thought was new.

"Nay," he said curtly, "Nay."

"Nay?" exclaimed the monk in seeming surprise. "Wert thou not then virgin knight?"

"For a year I dwelt in sin," said Anguish in a low voice.

"And thy lady knew this?" said the monk.

"Ay," said Anguish, and unbidden a deep flush overspread his face.

"Methinks she also had somewhat to forgive," said the monk quietly.

Tears were in his eyes and blurred the forest for a moment. His lips trembled in tenderness. Anguish was silent, staring hard at the trees.

"Thou art right," he said at last suddenly. "She knew my worst. I did not question her. She forgave me; to her I was merciless. When I see her again I will atone."

"When will that be?" said the monk quietly.

"I know not," said Anguish. "I left her at Camelot, without farewell, none knowing the truth. I thought never to look upon her face again; but now, methinks, one day I will go back—"

"And take her to thy heart?" said Brother Trestriste. His voice thrilled with longing, but Anguish did not heed.

"Nay," he answered frowning. "Forgive her I may; but I cannot take her to my heart."

"Ah, my son," said the monk, tenderly, sadly, "because thou hast lost thy saint, thine image of one who never was, thou must break the woman's heart. Anguish, Anguish, thou knowst not what love is!"

"And dost thou know?" said Anguish, somewhat petulantly. "Thou speakest strangely for a monk. Now tell me what love is, if thou dost know."

The monk sat silent, looking at his horse's head.

"Is it love," Anguish went on, "that is between Launcelot and Guenever?"

"Nay, it is lust," said Brother Trestriste quietly.

"Then is it love," continued Anguish, "that sways the lives of Tristram and my sister Isoud?"

"A passion—but no more yet," said the monk.

"Then what is love?" said Anguish curiously. They were riding now side by side.

The monk turned to him suddenly, and for a moment Anguish was visited again by a haunting memory whose source he could not tell, as the great blue eyes, shadowed with pain, were fixed upon his face.

"Thou wouldst not understand now, should I tell thee," said the monk gently; "and also, it could not be told. One day, Anguish, one day thou wilt know love."

There was a sudden rustle in the trees, a tumult breaking across the stillness of the forest. A knight in black armor, shouting defiance, rode out on the instant against Anguish. He was in the act of closing his visor, and at sight of his face the monk gave a sharp cry, and with sudden impulse spurred his palfrey. Anguish, taken by surprise, feutred his spear; but meanwhile the black knight, with an oath, dropped his spear and drew his sword upon Brother Trestriste, who had ridden directly in front of Anguish. The sword reached its aim. The monk fell with a groan, the blood streaming. Anguish, with a sharp exclamation of rage and dismay, called furiously on the knight to dismount.

The combat was short, but fierce. The two flew at each other like wode men, and it was not a half-hour ere Anguish had stretched the black knight dead upon the earth with a broken neck. Then regarding not his own wounds he ran to the monk.

Brother Trestriste lay in a faint on the ground, a deep wound in his shoulder. His horse, frightened by the combat, had fled into the forest; but Anguish's horse and that of the black knight were yet present and unwounded. Anguish, staunching the monk's blood in some rough wise, looked about him in despair. Through the hush, he heard of a sudden the chiming of a bell,

"Blessed be Jesu, some hermitage sure is nigh," he said to himself. "I will take him thither. Hermits are oft good leeches."

CHAPTER NINETEEN

The · Hermit's · Hut · · ·

A nguish, bearing the unconscious monk in his arms, and somewhat faint from his own wounds, staggered in the direction of the chiming bell. He had fortunately but a few rods to traverse from the scene of the combat ere he reached a tiny rustic chapel, with a hermit within reciting Vespers.

At sound of Anguish's clattering footsteps, he turned with a start, and hastened towards him, disclosing a meagre, kindly face, lit by large brown eyes.

"Brother," said Anguish, "here, as thou seest, is a holy man, sore wounded for my sake. I beseech thee, if thou hast any leechcraft, to use thy skill upon him."

The hermit responded with alacrity, and bade Anguish take Brother Trestriste into his hut, a fragrant leafy structure built just outside the chapel. Anguish carried in the monk with tenderness, and laid him down gently upon the hermit's couch.

"I were best alone with him," said the hermit. "Go without, fair son, and wait till I come to thee. Methinks the good brother is not wounded unto death."

Anguish went obediently. As he reached the low door, and bent his head to pass through it, the wounded monk stirred and threw out his arm.

"Anguish!" he breathed faintly; "Anguish!"

"Is that thy name?" asked the hermit, and as Anguish assented, he continued, "Be not troubled, noble knight. He knows not that he calls thee. He is but coming out of his swoon."

Anguish, reassured, passed on. As he disappeared, Brother Trestriste, sighing, opened his eyes, and looked with solemn wonder into the hermit's kindly face bent over him.

"Fear not, good brother," said the hermit. "Thou hast been hurt by some mischance, and I seek to heal thee. Prythee let me search thy wound."

The monk made a feeble gesture of protest.

"Nay," said the hermit soothingly, "beseech thee let me see thy hurt. I am skilled in leechcraft, and may heal thee by God's grace."

The monk shook his head as vigorously as his strength permitted. "Nay," he said; "nay, let be."

"Thy wound, perchance, is fatal," said the hermit, striving to alarm the monk; for he did not in truth think the wound mortal. Brother Trestriste smiled.

"So best," he said faintly, "to die for my lord Anguish—that were indeed for me the Beatific Vision."

The hermit looked at him startled, and somewhat shocked, deeming indeed that his wits wandered.

"Thou must love Sir Anguish well, brother," he said gravely. Then a bright thought occurred to him. "For his sake," he said persuasively, "for his sake let me search thy wound. He brought thee hither, sore distressed, beseeching me to heal thee."

The monk gave the faint shadow of a shrug, as if submitting to the inevitable. He grew white, and his eyes closed again. The hermit, with an exclamation of concern, brought water from a jar standing near, sprinkled it on the monk's face and held it to his lips. Then, having partly revived him, the kindly recluse removed the monkish dress without further ado, and disclosed a slender shoulder, white and tender, an ugly wound staining it deep-red.

The hermit looked at the soft flesh with surprise and a growing suspicion. Then, with a sudden impulse, he pushed down the robe still further and confirmed his thought. He paused in dismay.

Dieudonnée's senses were fast leaving her again, but she felt the movement, and the thought that followed it. With a violent effort, she recalled her straying wits, drew her monkish garments about her, and looked up into the horrified face of the hermit with all her heart in her appealing eyes.

"He knows not," she whispered. "Tell him not, of charity. Let me stay here with thee until I am healed, and then I will go. None need be told."

The hermit hesitated; but the passionately pleading face and the angry wound together decided his kindly heart. He nodded, and without a word began to bind up the shoulder. While he used ointment and bandages with skilful fingers, Dieudonnée, her heart content, made no further effort to chain her fluttering senses. It was a fragile-looking thing indeed, whiter than the white monkish garments, that lay limply at length before the hermit as he completed his task.

Anguish's step was shortly heard outside the hut.

"May I come in?" he called; and as the hermit assented, he entered. He looked horror-stricken as he saw Brother Trestriste lying in an inanimate heap upon the couch of leaves. "Is he dead?" he whispered.

"Nay," said the hermit, watching Anguish keenly. "He but swoons; and I think it well to leave him in the stupor for a while. Now for thine own wounds, fair son. Remove thine armor, prythee."

Anguish submitted himself to the hermit's hands; but watched the monk.

"What think'st thou of his wounds?" he asked at length.

"They are not mortal," replied the hermit cheerfully. "Natheless they are sufficient to keep him here for some months until he has fully recovered." He looked at Anguish sharply as he spoke, having still some faint suspicion whether the woman in the monk's garments had indeed told truth when she said that the knight knew not her sex.

Anguish looked reflective.

"That is as I feared," he said at length. "Then, by your leave, keep him in your care. Later, I will ride hither for him after I have achieved my quest."

"And what is thy quest, fair son?" said the hermit curiously.

Anguish crossed himself.

"I seek the vision of the Sangreal," he said reverently.

"God grant thee success," the hermit said, crossing himself also, and his latent suspicion vanishing forthwith. "Thou art right, fair son. The monk's wounds will keep him prisoner long, and he is safe with me. Go thou on thy quest."

A few hours later. Anguish, his wounds bound up and himself and his horse rested and refreshed, rode away from the hut. The hermit stood watching him, and sighed with relief as at last he disappeared.

"He does not know," he said to himself. "He would not so willingly have left her were she his leman. Jesu forbid that her sex be discovered by any other. For if 'twere, 'twould be a pretty coil for me."

Dieudonnée was tossing and murmuring in a kind of feeble delirium as he entered the hut. The hermit stood beside the couch and looked down at her.

"A fortnight will heal her," he said aloud. "I lied to the fair knight. He must not be kept back from that high and holy quest by any mere woman."

Dieudonnée opened her eyes and looked up at him with a wide and piteous gaze.

"Anguish!" she said. "Anguish! Ah, Jesu, where art thou? Isoud was right. God give thee love, my heart."

She smiled suddenly and tenderly; but an instant later she was babbling again disconnectedly. The hermit knelt in a corner of the hut, placidly telling his beads. Anguish, his heart bent on high and holy things, rode solitary through the forest, his erstwhile monkish companion for the time quite out of his recollection.

CHAPTER TWENTY

he • Vengeance • of • Anguish

A month after Anguish had left Brother Trestriste in the hermit's hut he was riding still, with nothing as yet achieved of his quest. He had eaten naught save bread and water, as commanded by the priest at Carbonek Castle; he had been shriven and houselled at every opportunity that had offered; the hair shirt he wore next his body; and yet he had come no nearer to realizing his hope than at the beginning of his quest.

Sometimes dreams came to him, he scarce knew whether in remembrance or in prophecy. Again the white dove bearing the golden censer fluttered across his slumbers. Occasionally the fair maiden clothed in snowy samite held aloft the white Mystery of the Grail. Several times the old man with the hoary beard sang again to his harp of Joseph of Armathie. But nothing more happened; and Anguish went blindly on his way, scarce knowing how his quest would end, sometimes scarce caring; wondering now and then what was indeed in store for him.

Of the monk he thought little. The hermit had told him that Brother Trestriste's wounds would require time and care; and Anguish felt that he was in good hands. Dieudonnée, on the contrary, persistently came into his mind. He dreamed of her by night; and sometimes the maiden in white samite bearing the Holy Grail seemed to have her face. When so it chanced, at dawn he woke and shuddered at the blasphemy. By day, in his solitary rides, despite himself he saw her continually in his mind's eye; now the Dieudonnée he had imagined and idealized, pale saint with golden hair; now the trembling woman in whose eyes he had first read love the day he had been victor of the tournament for her sake; yet again, the figure of despair who had confessed to him the morning of their wedding. Sometimes she was none of these; but a Dieudonnée he had never seen in life, with eyes that reproached but lips that trembled into a smile that he knew was for him alone. Where was she, and what did she at Camelot?

Once it struck cold across his remembrance that she had told him she would not be at Camelot when he returned. What had she meant? At the time he had heeded the words little, caring naught. But now—and puzzling over the problem, he recollected with a start the quest on which he was bound, and wondered frowning whether the thought of Dieudonnée was what kept him from achieving his high adventure.

And so, as the days passed, and the Vision was not yet his, there grew upon Anguish a deep discouragement. Helplessly he prayed to be worthy, and yet he seemed no nearer worthiness. At length, one evening at sunset, he saw the towers of the White Abbey, and therein sought shelter and refreshment.

All that night, instead of sleeping, he knelt solitary in prayer. The place was empty and silent, unlit save for the burning lamp before the altar. There Anguish kept his vigil and searched his heart, and the pale dawn found him still upon his knees.

That night of silence brought him no vision, no light upon his way; but when the monks entered in the early morn they found him kneeling at the altar, his eyes upon the crucifix, his hands crossed upon his breast. So he remained motionless throughout the service. At its conclusion, he spoke in a low voice to the Abbot as the monks were leaving the chapel, and besought him to remain.

When the place was again empty and silent. Anguish said to the Abbot:

"Father, I beseech thee, receive me here a novice among thy monks."

The Abbot looked at him astonished.

"A novice?" he repeated. "Thou? Gladly, my son, an it be thy vocation; but bethink thee well."

Anguish looked at him wearily.

"I am a prince," he said, "son of the King of Ireland. I am a knight of Arthur's court, and I have sought the Sangreal and found it not. Moreover, I am a great sinner, and life is no longer sweet. Receive me here, and let me live and die a holy man."

The Abbot hesitated. Anguish waited silently for a reply, his tired eyes upon the altar. Suddenly, breaking the stillness, they heard without the abbey walls the clear winding of a horn.

"Some hunting-party seeks refuge here," said the Abbot hastily, relieved at the interruption. "I must go to welcome them. For thy words, son, fast and pray, and reflect earnestly. Then if it be still thy desire to become a monk, I shall with joy receive thee. But such matters must not be settled hastily."

He signed the cross upon Anguish's forehead, and left him. Anguish heard in the distance the opening and shutting of the great outer doors, the entrance of the hunting-party with joyous noise and clatter. He hoped dully that none would come to the chapel. An instant later he heard the Abbot speaking just without, and mingling with his voice another, frank and gay.

"Ay," it said; "the chase was hot yesterday; and ere starting out again, we came hither to crave thy hospitality. We cannot tarry long. Leave me awhile with Prince Anguish; and later he and I will break our fast together."

The Abbot acquiesced in a low voice. Anguish turned, and came face to face with Tristram of Cornwall. Into the dim incense-haunted chapel, the newcomer entering, seemed to carry a breath of joyous life, a memory and hope of spring.

"Anguish, Anguish," Tristram cried, clasping his hand. "Ah, it is a happy fate that brought me here this morn! Come, man, come out with me into the day! We cannot talk here without irreverence." He made a hasty genuflection to the altar. "Where hast thou been? What hast thou achieved? Isoud asks through me. She told me also, if I saw thee, to inquire particularly as to the welfare of that holy monk who letters brought to her from Queen Guenever."

Anguish followed him. A few moments later they were pacing together the garden paths of the Abbey.

"Thou art pale, man," said Tristram, after Anguish had briefly answered his questions. "Thou lookest white and worn. Thou didst pray before the altar all last night? Tush! Nay, now, I mean no irreverence; but thou art neither monk nor priest. Instead of praying, thou shouldst be fighting for God and thy lady."

"I have no lady," said Anguish shortly.

"Then find one," answered Tristram gaily. "The rarest lady in all the world is mine, thy sister Isoud. But there are others beautiful, although not peerless. If thou hast no lady, seek her. It is thy duty. Somewhere she waits for thee."

Anguish was silent. For an instant in his thought Dieudonnée's sad eyes reproached his denial of her.

Tristram stooped and plucked a rose from a bush near by; then tossed it to Anguish, smiling.

"Take that, and with it go to seek her who shall be thy rose of the world."

Anguish, with sudden passion, crushed the flower cruelly in his hand and flung it from him, a bruised mass. Tristram looked at him, startled.

"Anguish! That was no knightly deed. What meanst thou? Scorn not love so mightily, or love may scorn thee. What is this tale that the Abbot breathed in my ear awhile since that thou wouldst become a monk?"

"That is my desire," said Anguish briefly, shutting his lips determinedly.

Tristram laughed lightly.

"A dream," he said; "a boy's dream! A year of it, and thou wouldst eat out thy heart with longing for freedom. Come, Anguish, come with me, and follow the hunt to-day. I go with Isoud shortly to Arthur's Court. Best join us."

Anguish shook his head.

"At least then, come with us on the hunt," said Tristram. "Hark! Methinks I hear the welcome chiming of the refectory bell. Come, break thy fast with me. Anguish, thou art young. Spend not thy life on pale prayers. Live, live, and love! For me, I am a lover, and as a lover I would live and die. Isoud—ah, name of joy and all delight!" He bent his head at the word. "For Isoud's sake, come with me into life," he said; and smiled.

An hour later, Tristram and Anguish left the abbey together. Tristram had so far prevailed. Anguish had not relinquished his desire; but he had consented to wait. He rode a few rods with Tristram and his hunting-party; then left them and once more pursued his solitary way. After he had been on the high road some hours he came suddenly on what seemed familiar ground. He realized presently why. He was on the border-land of the Castle of Hellayne.

When this knowledge came to him he mused a space. Launcelot, he remembered, had bidden him to take vengeance himself one day. Now was the time and perchance the hour. Yet—since he was bound on the quest of the Sangreal, should he turn aside from it for anything so earthly as this vengeance, this memory of his year of shame? But she was an evil woman; his cause was just. She had blighted his life; she still lived to ruin others. Pressing his lips together, he made his decision and spurred his horse.

It was with little effort that he overcame the various knights guarding her castle. He was no longer a maiden warrior, and his arm was both swift and sure. Finally, he rode furiously into the courtyard, and called upon Hellayne to come forth.

The damosel of the golden shield appeared instead in response, and when she saw him she began to laugh mockingly.

"Good Lord!" she said. "This old toy of my mistress's has come back! What ails thee, boy? Wouldst try again the air of Hellayne's castle?"

"I will not speak with thee," replied Anguish curtly. "Send hither thy mistress."

The maiden disappeared, and an instant later Hellayne came in her stead.

"Prince Anguish!" she exclaimed in a tone of surprise and pleasure. "Prythee alight, my lord."

"I am not come for soft pleasures, madam," replied Anguish; "but rather to give thee the judgment of God."

She went white, feeling that he no longer spoke as a boy; but she smiled still.

"Prythee, enter," she reiterated.

"I will do so; but not as thy guest," said Anguish.

The great doors were flung open for him at Hellayne's command. Anguish entered the hall, and at its end Hellayne stood on the dais, smiling at him. Anguish approached her, gripping his sword; but even as he did so he felt as when he had been before in this place, that his senses were growing curiously misty. He strove to hold them despairingly; but as he reached the dais he put his hand to his head uncertainly.

Hellayne with a smile of triumph advanced a step. At that moment the hall doors were flung open violently; and a slender monk rushed up the hall towards Anguish.

"Sir Anguish, Sir Anguish," he called clearly; "prythee bethink thee! She bewitches thee even now. Bid her come without the walls, and there accomplish thy vengeance."

Hellayne gave a savage exclamation. But the monk's words were enough. Anguish recovered himself on the instant.

"Come with me, madam," he said curtly to Hellayne.

She began to exclaim and protest, meanwhile sending signals to her minions to take the monk captive. But Anguish's thoughts were quick and clear.

"Follow me close, Brother Trestriste," he said. "Lady Hellayne, lead the way to the battlements."

She had grown white, feeling that her power over him was gone. Her servants began to weep, and most of them to make their escape. When at length Anguish reached the outer air with Hellayne and the monk, no other was near.

"Thine hour has come," he said to her, and drew his sword. "Pray."

"Nay," she answered defiantly. "I will not whine at death. Before thou slayest me let me say one word."

"Say it," he replied.

"Knowst thou who the black knight was that thou didst kill there yonder in the forest near the hermit's hut?" she asked.

Anguish had lifted his sword. He paused.

"Tell me," he said.

"Ask thy lady," said Hellayne, and laughed. "Find out the rest. Thy vengeance is complete. Let the sword fall."

She laughed again, and Anguish's sword cut short the sound.

"Bear witness, brother," said Anguish gravely to the monk, looking down at the dead body; "bear witness that this was a righteous slaying. Come now. My work here is done."

They left the empty courtyard, mounted their horses, and rode away together. As they reached the high road. Anguish looked at the monk anxiously.

"Thy wounds are quite healed?" he asked.

"Ay," said the monk quietly; "they have been healed this fortnight, and since I have been riding to find thee. The hermit told me that Hellayne's castle was not far away, and there I knew thou wouldst go sooner or later."

"How didst thou know that?" said Anguish surprised. The monk shrugged his shoulders.

"Monks learn things in many ways," he answered; "and now, tell me my son, hast yet achieved thy quest?"

Anguish shook his head sadly.

"Tell me why it is that I do not, brother," he said mournfully. "I have in all things done as I was told. I eat bread and water, and naught else. I confess me oft, and partake frequently of the Blessed Sacrament. A hair shirt I wear ever against my body. Is it that I am not sinless? Surely I have atoned. My year with Hellayne was sore fleshly sin indeed and yet—"

"Methinks that alone would not hinder thee," said Brother Trestriste.

"Galahad, it is true, is sinless, and Percivale," said Anguish sorrowfully. "It has seemed to me of late, brother, that perchance this quest is not for me. I consider now entering the cloister, and there striving to atone my sins by prayer and fast and vigil."

"My son, my son," said the monk suddenly, the words breaking from him with a cry, "meseems thy fault is not that sin of thy eager boyhood, but rather that thy thought is of thyself, and not of God. If it be merely to save thine own soul that thou goest on this quest, be sure thou shalt never achieve it; but if with a pure heart and a clean conscience thou seekest the Vision for the glory of God—"

He paused. Anguish's eyes were fixed upon his face. The monk's voice dropped to its deepest note, and he went on, rather to himself than to Anguish.

"Meseems, also," he said, "that to forgive much—to love much—shall we not all so find the love of God, and the Vision of His Presence?"

Anguish drew a long breath. "Thy words pierce my heart," he said. "It is true. A new hope comes to me from thee. I will pray God for His grace to lead me upon this path that thou hast shown."

CHAPTER TWENTY-ONE

Love · and · Death

Three years after the slaying of Hellayne, Anguish and Brother Trestriste sat together in the forest. Both were pale and lean and ill-clad. Their horses were mere sorry nags. Anguish's golden shield was bent and battered with the dents of many a combat. The monk's white garments were scarcely more than rags, soiled and travel stained.

Anguish sat, his chin on his hand, gazing thoughtfully into the tangled maze of the forest. Joy was no longer in his face; the ardor of youth was gone forever. Instead there dwelt upon it a marvellous peace. The monk sat somewhat behind the knight, his hands clasped lightly together. His great eyes were no less sombre than of old; but in the emaciated outlines of face and form there was visible an infinite and touching patience.

Anguish broke the silence at length.

"I have sought long and vainly," he said. "It is not for me, brother. God denies me the desire of my heart. His will be done. The Vision is for holier eyes than mine."

The monk made no audible reply. He smiled at Anguish, wistfully, tenderly. Anguish silently put out his hand, and the monk clasped it close. The knight gazed again into the forest's green labyrinth with a look of renunciation. "The dream is over," he said; "I must tomorrow back to Camelot."

A deep flush overspread the monk's face.

"Wherefore?" he said.

"Because," answered Anguish quietly, "because I am yet a knight; and if it is not vouchsafed me to serve God in the holiest way, I may in one more earthly. And moreover—"

He paused and smiled. The monk's heart beat fast.

"Moreover," Anguish went on in a lower voice, "I have tarried long from my wife, and I would go back to her."

The monk's hand trembled in Anguish's palm.

"Thou wert right," Anguish continued; "and Isoud was right, and Tristram. God gives us naught better in this poor world than love. I thank thee for thy farewell wish, Isoud; and I thank God that it is realized. Where art thou now, my sister? Shall I ever see thee more?"

"Thou dost—love thy wife then?" said Brother Trestriste in a low voice.

Anguish bent his head.

"But she is a sinful woman," said the monk wistfully. He was very pale, and his great eyes besought. But Anguish did not see.

"What matter?" he answered. "She is mine, and I am hers; so out of all the world. It is enough. 'Tis strange. These years during which I have sought to purify me and to atone my sins by gentle thoughts and high endeavor that I might win the Sangreal— these years instead have brought me—love."

"And now?" said the monk softly.

"Now," answered Anguish, "God who is good hath sent me love; and I love my lady and hold her close in my thought with neither shame nor reproach. My lady —saint or sinner, true or faithless, living or dead—mine through time and eternity, forever mine."

The monk gave a long tremulous sigh of infinite content, and gently drew his hand away. He clasped it with its fellow, and raised to heaven his thin face, transfigured for an instant with perfect joy. As he lowered his eyes he gave a start.

"A man comes through the forest!"

Anguish seized his sword from where it lay beside him on the turf and rose. But as the newcomer approached, the knight's face changed from watchfulness to recognition, and then to anxiety.

"It is the messenger that Isoud always sends," he said. "Can aught be wrong?"

He advanced to meet the man, who in a moment was at his feet. The messenger was almost exhausted, and had scarcely strength to hand the letter he carried to Anguish ere he sank in a nerveless heap. The monk ran to a spring nearby for water. While he refreshed the messenger. Anguish hastily read the letter.

"How long hast thou been finding me?" he said at length shortly, so absorbed in the news the messenger had brought that his condition went unnoticed.

"Many months, my lord," the man answered. "I knew not where to find thee; and oft I reached a place just after thou hadst departed."

Anguish groaned and placed a hand to his brow.

"Mayhap the worst may have chanced," he said. Then of a sudden, awakening to the messenger's plight, he leaned over him gently. "Good fellow," he said, "good fellow! I blame thee not; and I must not leave thee to perish. Come, I will carry thee in front of me on my horse, and take thee to the nearest abbey. Then—" he turned to the monk and spoke passionately—"then to Cornwall with utmost speed."

The monk looked at him anxiously, but did not speak. Anguish glanced at the messenger, who by this time seemed to have lapsed entirely into unconsciousness, and said in a low voice:

"Isoud calls me to come to her. She fears King Mark, whose jealousy grows apace—and if her brother is near her, she hopes to dull his suspicions.

We will leave this faithful man in some safe refuge, and then God grant we are in time."

The monk's heart gave a throb of joy. Anguish had evidently no thought of leaving Brother Trestriste behind.

"As thou wilt, my lord," he said.

A few hours later the two were galloping side by side in silence. Suddenly Anguish spoke. "Camelot must wait," he said. "Isoud needs now my knighthood; and my lady—"

He paused. The monk answered softly: "Thy lady, as I do, would bid thee go." The night had been a dream of exquisite moonlight; and as Anguish and the monk alighted in early morn at the door of King Mark's castle, the cloudless sky was paling into dawn's unearthly beauty. A sleepy porter admitted them; and a messenger was sent to tell the king and queen of their arrival.

Anguish and Brother Trestriste stood in the courtyard waiting. The castle yet slept while the earth awakened; and only the twitter of drowsy birds broke the silence. Nearby lay, Anguish knew, the garden that Isoud loved. They could see from where they stood the tops of the trees that bordered it; and ever and anon the morning breeze swept through them with a soft, long sigh.

As time passed, and the messenger did not return, Anguish grew restless.

"I shall wait no longer," he said at last, his voice, sharp with impatience, jarring on the quiet air. "Come, brother, let us to Isoud's garden. I know the way. There we will wait until the castle wakes; and then receive King Mark's ungracious welcome and Isoud's loving greeting."

He started without more ado, and the monk followed quietly. They passed from the courtyard into the garden by means of a secret gate in the heavy wall, the spring of which Anguish knew. In a moment they were among the trees. Anguish led the way with surety.

"We will go to the sun-dial," he said. "Isoud loves it well, and I have often sat with her near it. Then we shall know, too, when it is time to return to the castle."

As they left the trees and entered the garden's wilderness of bloom Anguish started.

"Isoud is already there," he said. He went a step or two further; then paused. There were two figures by the sun-dial.

He hesitated, then advanced slowly, the monk following. The glow of sunrise was just beyond the sundial, and threw the outlines of Tristram and Isoud into strong relief. Isoud's hands, clasped in Tristram's, were held to his heart; her face was uplifted to his. As Anguish came still nearer, Tristram bent to kiss her; and on the instant she was in his arms.

"The stars have paled," Anguish heard him murmur; "the cruel sun brings day."

"Ah, no, night has fallen," she answered. "In its gloom I rest till thou dost come back to me."

A twig snapped under Anguish's foot, and the two started apart. On the instant another figure rose behind them, dark and sinister against the sunrise light. Tristram and Isoud did not see. Then of a sudden a sword was driven vengefully from behind straight through Tristram's body. He sank without a groan, instantly killed; and King Mark stood frowning above him.

Isoud, her eyes large, her face white, made no sound. She stood staring at her dead lover, blind to all else. Anguish ran towards her with a cry. Her eyes still fixed on Tristram's face, she crept waveringly across the narrow space that divided them; stood an instant stiffly upright; then suddenly fell prone across his body, and with one great sob, gave forth her soul.

Tristram's harp, twined with red roses, lay on the ground nearby. King Mark seized it furiously, and tore its strings asunder. They sounded jarring discords. Then with a savage laugh, he flung it down, and crashed away through the bushes.

Anguish knelt, the tears streaming down his face. He lifted the ruined harp, and touched it gently.

"King Mark did well," he muttered. "No hand could touch Tristram's harp into sweetness e'er again."

The day had fully dawned; and to welcome its beauty the birds broke forth into musical, exultant chorus. Thus in joy and life was sung the requiem of Tristram and Isoud.

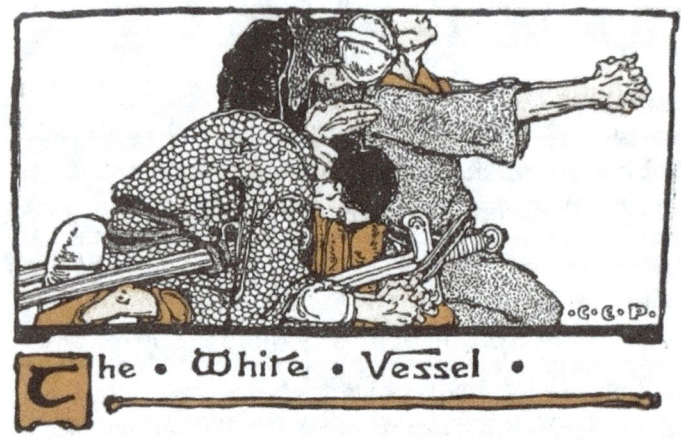

CHAPTER TWENTY-TWO

The • White • Vessel •

A thunder-storm was raging when Anguish and Brother Trestriste left King Mark's castle together. The day of unearthly beauty upon which Tristram and Isoud died had been succeeded on the following morning by a howling tempest which had lasted ever since. Anguish, enduring King Mark's grudging hospitality, had stayed long enough to see that his sister had all the proper rites and that Tristram received honorable burial. As in a dream he had performed his duties; and the ceremonies at last ended, he took to horse, despite the yet raging storm.

The celebrant of Isoud's funeral mass had sung it tremulously and with tenderness. The priest was an old man who had come with Isoud from Ireland, and had known her as a child. A sterner man, or one who had not known her, might have denounced her death and its manner, and refused to give her Christian burial. But no one who knew Isoud could, it seemed, do otherwise than love her.

In the raging storm, at length, monk and knight rode away. They made their way rapidly, for the most part in silence. They had fallen into the habit of silence, these two, when alone together, oft understanding each other without speech. But when for a day they had ridden through the driving rain, and it still showed no signs of abating, Anguish spoke.

"How wild the night," he said, "how tempest-tossed the forest! Methinks, perchance, that on the wings of the storm ride the free spirits of Tristram and Isoud, together now forever."

"It may be," answered the monk, lifting his pale face to the tempest. "She is gone. Their two souls have journeyed forth together. Wish them no better fate."

At morn the tempest broke. It chanced that at sunrise they reached the seaside; and dismounted to rest a while before pursuing their journey further. As they waited in silence, looking out across the restless waves, the monk suddenly touched Anguish upon the shoulder.

"See yonder, my lord, what vessel is that?" he said.

Anguish looked and started. A ship was sailing towards them all covered with white samite so fast that it seemed flying. Anguish crossed himself in the midst of his forehead, incredulous joy upon his face.

"Fair Jesu," he breathed; "fair Jesu, hast thou granted indeed to me, a sinful man—"

The ship came nearer, landed. It seemed steered and sailed by invisible hands; and in its midst Anguish saw two knights, with faces familiar although not seen for long. He fell upon his knees.

"Galahad and Percivale," he breathed. "Ah, gracious Lord, what is this?"

The knights, also recognizing him, smiled in greeting.

"Come with us, Anguish," they called to him. "Ye be welcome. We have abiden you long. We marvel how ye came hither but if Our Lord brought you hither Himself."

"Certes, methinks He did," said Anguish half aloud. He rose from his knees, as in a dream, and crossing his hands on his breast, entered the ship. But his foot upon the deck, he turned and looked back. Brother Trestriste had knelt upon the shore, and waited motionless. Anguish looked wistfully from him to the two knights.

"I may take with me this holy man who hath been with me these many months throughout my quest?" he said.

Percivale looked doubtful; but Galahad replied:

"Nay, if the monk be worthy, and if it be God*s will that he come with us, the vessel will wait his boarding it. If not, it will go without him."

"Then if it be the latter," said Anguish suddenly and strongly, "if it be the latter, ye sail also without me."

"Come hither, my good brother," said Galahad gently.

The monk rose, his face white and shining, his hands crossed upon his breast, his eyes fixed upon Anguish in passionate love and faith. The vessel waited motionless. An instant later. Brother Trestriste knelt trembling in a comer of the deck, and the white ship sped once more across the restless sea.

The three knights, Galahad, Percivale and Anguish, sat in the hall of the Castle of Carbonek at the table of King Pelles. Through many strange adventures had they come, much pain endured and noble deeds performed, and now King Pelles received them with joy, knowing that they had fulfilled the quest of the Sangreal.

No one was with them save King Pelles and his son, and the monk, Brother Trestriste, kneeling humbly in the corner of the hall. All were silent, all waiting in great faith and lowliness, feeling that their quest was nigh its close.

Anon, of a sudden, through the stillness, alit a voice among them.

"They that ought not to sit at the table of Jesu Christ arise, for now shall very knights be fed."

There was an instant's pause. The knights looked from one to the other, and at King Pelles. The monk made as if to rise; then sank back, bowing his head. None moved further and the voice spoke again.

"There be two among you that be not in quest of the Sangreal," it said. "Therefore depart ye."

King Pelles and his son arose softly, and left the hall. They closed the door quietly behind them, and again a great silence filled the place.

Then, while they waited still, there grew gradually throughout the vast spaces of the hall a soft and tender light. With one accord the three knights fell upon their knees. The light grew brighter, more pervading; and suddenly in its radiance appeared four angels bearing a chair in which sat the aged man of Anguish's vision, clad in likeness of a bishop. Then the knights saw the table of silver with the Sangreal upon it; and around it the angels knelt. The Bishop knelt also, and made signs as if he were going to the sacring of the Mass. And at the Elevation they beheld a Figure in the likeness of a child, bright and shining, which smote itself into the Bread. When the Mass was ended the aged man approached Sir Galahad, where he knelt with the others, and kissed him.

"Kiss now thy fellows," he said; and Galahad obeyed. Then the old man said, "Servants of Christ Jesu, now ye shall be fed with such sweetmeats that never knight tasted."

Then of a sudden he vanished. The knights knelt still, in mingled dread and hope, and made their prayers. And again they heard a Voice like none earthly—

"My knights, and my servants, and my true children," it said, "which be come out of deadly sin into spiritual life, I will now no longer hide me from you, but ye shall see a part of my secrets and of my hidden things. Now hold and receive the high meat which ye have so much desired."

They felt, but saw not, a mysterious Presence in their midst; the Holy Vessel moved towards them, borne by invisible hands. The three knights waited in ecstasy of faith. First Galahad received his Saviour; then Percivale and Anguish. And when it was ended they knelt still, caught away from earth for a little space, and dwelling indeed in Paradise.

After a time the Voice spoke again.

"This night the vessel shall depart from this realm, and nevermore be seen here. They of this land be turned to evil living; wherefore I shall disherit them of the honor which I have done them. Go ye all tomorrow unto the sea, where ye shall find your ship ready. One of you shall die in my service, but two of you shall come again."

The Voice paused; and when once more it spoke, it was in blessing. At the conclusion of the great Name of the Trinity the three knights crossed themselves devoutly. The light grew brighter, more unearthly, blinding in its radiance. The three knights bent their heads and closed their eyes. When, an instant later, they opened them again the hall was empty and silent, and gone the heavenly light.

CHAPTER TWENTY-THREE

The Passing of Dagonet

L auncelot stood at the door of his tent, his arms folded, gazing quietly into space. Around him were noise and turmoil; soldiers running to and fro on various camp duties, flinging rough jests at each other; armed men clattering up and down on horseback and on foot; all the numberless sights and sounds of preparation for battle. But from all this bustle Launcelot seemed curiously remote. He alone was still amid the tumult; he stood solitary, aloof from the crowd.

Of a sudden he saw the numberless groups around him turn towards one centre. Idly his gaze followed them; then, with an exclamation, he made a step forward. Coming through the throng he beheld a knightly figure followed by a monk. This alone would have been too common a sight to awaken the interest of the camp; but as the two strangers pursued their way Launcelot noticed that a curious hush fell upon the multitude. Why? He at once recognized Anguish of Ireland, grown older and more weary; the monk's features he noted little; but there was about both something that for an instant held the careless crowds in awe. He saw one rough fellow cross himself. Another fell upon his knees.

"Anguish," he cried, as the knight neared him, extending both hands, "Anguish, it has been long since I have seen thee."

Anguish's face lit with pleasure. Launcelot noticed that the bustle of the camp had renewed itself, now that the strangers had passed. The three went within the tent together.

"Ay, it has been many months," Anguish answered simply; "and I have not come now to abide with thee, Sir Launcelot. Afterwards—but now I am bound on a quest."

He paused an instant; then added in a low voice: "'Tis the third quest on which I have been bound; and God knoweth it means much to me. Sir Launcelot, canst tell me aught of Lady Dieudonnée?"

Launcelot looked at him wonderingly, with some reproach, and shook his head.

"I left her on our wedding-morn," said Anguish; "and since then I have known naught of her. Now I am newly come from witnessing Galahad's death, and the departure of the Holy Vessel into heaven—"

Launcelot gazed at him in awe mingled with envy.

"Then hast thou achieved the Sangreal," he whispered; "and Galahad, my son, is dead. Oh, blessed are ye both among men! Oft have I sought to behold that holy Vision, but dwelling in sin, I was not worthy."

"God granted it to me," said Anguish, reverently; "and unto it I might not be disobedient; else should I have long since sought my wife. Twice I have been on my way to her; and both times—thou knowest, then, naught of her?"

Launcelot's "Nay" was interrupted; for suddenly the noisy camp was filled with an added tumult of laughter and loud shouting. Launcelot, frowning, rose and glanced without; then hastily beckoned to Anguish.

As they stood looking out together, they saw a figure, familiar, although not seen for long, dancing fantastically towards them through the crowd. He was tall and very thin, and grimaced cheerfully at the screaming people as he came. But ever and anon, he seemed to stumble, and as he approached more nearly, they saw that his face was drawn and pitiful despite the jester's grin. Anguish cried out, "Dagonet!" and at the name, the monk sprang up and looked out also at the fantastic figure. In a moment Dagonet was at their feet with the ghost of a chuckle.

"Good-morrow, good death," he muttered, as if saluting one unseen. Then he drew a letter from his bosom, and gave it to Launcelot.

"From the holy abbess Guenever at Almesbury," he said; and grimaced again.

Launcelot, without a word, opened the letter quietly. The jester sat back on his heels and grinned up at Anguish and the monk.

"Thou hast seen much—and yet how blind thou art!" he said to Anguish.

Anguish smiled.

"Thou speakest sooth," he said. "Would that my eyes were keen enough to find one path for which my spirit yearns—the way to my lady!"

He turned aside with a smothered groan. Launcelot was absorbed in his letter. For an instant the jester's eyes inquired, the monk's appealing ones bade nay.

Launcelot folded the letter and sighed.

"I will answer send," he said slowly. "Tell me, Dagonet, where is Arthur now?"

The jester shrugged.

"Who knows?" he said. "Mordred lords it on his throne; and for my Uncle Arthur—Sir Bedivere tells a tale of a magic barge, and of queens therein, lamenting sore, who carried away the king with them to dwell in the Isle of Avilion and heal him of his grievous wound. Would that he had taken me with him!" His voice fell into a plaintive whine. "My Uncle Merlin, too, has gone away forever into the forest shadows. I have not been very merry lately with my Uncle Merlin and my Uncle Arthur gone."

Launcelot set his lips. "Mordred must be punished," he said. "For that I make preparation."

"Where dwells Queen Guenever?" asked Anguish abruptly, struck with a new thought.

"At Almesbury," answered Dagonet, clasping his hands with an air of piety and rolling his eyes to heaven."She queens it no longer, but is a holy abbess. Thither hath she fled with five of her ladies."

"Ah!" said Anguish, with a sudden hope. He looked at Dagonet eagerly. "Canst remember their names?" he said.

Dagonet appeared stupid on the instant.

"They are dead to the world," he answered mincingly; "and their worldly names are dead with them."

"Dead to the world," repeated Anguish with a quick fear. "Perchance then—" he looked at Launcelot. "I will to Almesbury," he said. "Mayhap there I shall learn tidings of my lady."

"It is well resolved," Launcelot answered gently.

Dagonet lay panting in a comer of the vessel, and beside him knelt Brother Trestriste. The passage from France to England had proved a stormy one; and Anguish doubted much whether the enfeebled jester would survive it. He had been very weak on reaching Launcelot's camp, but he insisted on leaving it with them, and on leaving it at once. Now it was near sunset, and an hour more would see them safely landed on England's coast.

Anguish stood with the steersman, his thoughts with Dieudonnée. Strangely, he had no fear that he would not find her at last. While dwelling with the Sangreal the accidents of earth had for a time so completely left his thought that he scarcely reckoned with them now. He had been long on his way to her—ah, she would know why, and forgive! Neither Isoud's cry for help nor the holy summons of the Sangreal would she have had him ignore. She would understand. And if in this life he might not reach her, then in eternity—

He looked at the feeble jester, and his thoughts took a new turn. Alack, how sad a thing it was to see merriment perish! He recollected Arthur's court in its gaiety, now past; and it seemed to him that the dying fool in faded motley represented its present desolation. He turned and looked out sadly across the sea. Presently he heard the jester speak; but he did not catch the words, nor the monk's reply.

"Oh, holy man, holy man, wilt hear my confession?" was what Dagonet said. He smiled at Brother Trestriste whimsically. The monk flushed.

"I am no priest," he answered in a low voice.

"Confess then to me," said the jester. He lifted himself with an effort, and breathed softly in Brother Trestriste's ear. "Dear lady, is all well with thee?"

It was the first time he had put into words his knowledge of her identity.

For answer she looked at him steadily, gravely.

"He loves thee," Dagonet said low, voicing her expression. "'Tis enough. And now—out there across the sea methinks one comes to meet me—fool skeleton with grinning jaws—like me."

He wreathed his face into his customary grimace; then the ghastly distortion died away, and he looked at her quietly.

"Life's jest is ended," he said. "Lady, before I die, wilt let me kiss thy hand—as if I were knight, not fool?"

From his small gray eyes, for an instant, a soul looked forth, pathetic and alone. Dieudonnée sobbed.

"Nay," she said. "Instead—this." And, with a quick movement, she bent towards him impulsively, and kissed him on the forehead.

His face fell into lines of peace; his eyes closed; he sighed. Then of a sudden, ere she was aware, he staggered to his feet, and pointed across the sea with a cry.

"My Uncle Arthur!" he called clearly. "My Uncle Arthur! Then thou hast not forgot me in that fair Isle of Avilion! Thou couldst not live e'en there without thy poor fool to make thee merry! I come, I come!"

He drew something from his breast with a quick movement and flung it on the deck. The next instant he was poised lightly on the side of the vessel, his arms stretched towards the western glow. Anguish rushed towards him. Then—into the path of the sunset Dagonet plunged, and the waves closed above him.

at • Almesbury • • •

Vespers were being sung when Anguish and the monk reached Almesbury next day. A white-faced, frightened novice admitted them, trembling when she saw the mailed knight; and when asked whether they might see the queen, nodded and said ay, at the conclusion of the service.

She came to them at length, moving as stately in her nun's habit of black and white as formerly in her queenly robes of divers shining hues. Anguish, who had risen with the monk when he heard her approaching footsteps, started as he saw her garb. It was true he knew that she had retired to the cloister; but actually to see Launcelot's lady and Arthur's queen in the dull colors of a heavenly bride gave him a strange feeling betwixt surprise and pain. When the monk heard the queen coming he slipped quietly behind the arras, where he might see and not be seen. It seemed to him, watching Guenever keenly, that for an instant there flashed across the queen's face, as she saw Anguish's involuntary start of surprise, a gleam of her old delight in the power of her beauty.

"Prince Anguish!" said the queen, and the tears rushed to her eyes. The monk remembered that they ever had been wont to flow easily. "Come back after all these years? Ah, there have been great changes— where hast thou been?"

Anguish briefly recounted his adventures, purposely omitting for the moment his recent interview with Launcelot. When he mentioned his achievement of the Sangreal the queen crossed herself piously and lifted her beautiful eyes to heaven with a rapt look. An instant later she inquired gently for Isoud. Anguish frowned, sure that she must have heard of his sister's end; but perforce he mentioned it briefly.

"She died in sin," Guenever murmured, bending her head. She extended her hand to Anguish and lifted her tearful dark eyes to his. "My prayers and those of my nuns shall bespeak daily hereafter the safety of her soul."

Anguish did not touch her extended hand.

"I thank you, madam," he answered coldly. "It behooves us all to pray for departed souls; and therefore I pray for Tristram and Isoud; but methinks their souls, brave in love, stand as even a chance of winning heaven as either mine or thine."

Involuntarily he put his hand into his breast. The letter was there which Launcelot had sent in reply to Guenever and which Dagonet had flung upon the deck ere he leaped into the sea. But Anguish was not quite ready to give it to the queen.

"And whither goest thou now, Prince Anguish?" said the queen.

"I know not of a surety my future movements," he answered evasively; then added with more eagerness than he had displayed as yet, "Prythee, madam, of your charity tell me one thing. Which of your ladies are in attendance upon you here?"

The arras stirred slightly; but neither Anguish nor Guenever observed the movement.

"There are five in the company," she answered with some surprise; "Lynette and Argente, Anglides and Clarysyn and Feleloyle."

Anguish, hanging breathless on each name, sighed with disappointment as she reached the last.

"Then," he said, looking appealingly at the queen, "then, since she is not with thee, tell me, madam, where is my wife, whom I left with thee at Camelot long since? Thou wert wont to have her much about thee, since she was of Cameliard, thy birthplace. Tell me, then, where is Dieudonnée?"

The queen looked at him, startled, perplexed. In her new habit of sanctity it came haltingly to her lips to tell the old whim by which, mainly to rid herself of eyes that she felt saw into her own soul too keenly, she had sent his wife with him as a monk on a love journey. Moreover, she had taken it for granted that the sex of Brother Trestriste would be discovered shortly; nor had she thought of the matter for many months, being too busied with her own affairs. It flashed upon her now that the monk might be dead, and if so, Anguish might blame her for the death. She paltered with his question.

"Hast never seen her since?" she said.

Anguish looked at her sharply.

"Never," he said sternly. "Where is she?"

"I know not," said the queen, speaking truth.

Anguish made a step towards her; then restrained himself. "Where didst last hear of her?" he said.

Again the queen hesitated. Brother Trestriste came from behind the arras. At sight of him the queen gave an exclamation of strong surprise. The monk's eyes were fixed upon her, and compelled her as of yore.

"Where is my wife?" repeated Anguish.

"Ask the monk," said Guenever, half fearfully, half defiantly.

"The monk?" repeated Anguish questioningly.

Brother Trestriste put his hand on Anguish's shoulder with a light, tremulous touch.

"Thou hast never yet asked me," he said. "And I could have counseled thee long since. Let us go to Camelot, to the rose-bower. Perchance they are in ruins; but there, I promise thee, thou shalt find thy lady."

Anguish looked at him with incredulous joy.

"Speakest thou very sooth?" he said.

"I know whereof I speak," the monk answered. "And I promise thee, thou longest not more to find thy lady than she longs to be found."

Anguish drew a long breath, and turned as if to go, forgetful of all else. Then, suddenly recollecting himself, he drew from his breast Launcelot's letter and gave it to the queen.

"Dagonet was its bearer," he said; "but Dagonet is dead."

The queen, flushing with joy, opened the letter hastily. She did not heed the farewell of Anguish and the monk. But ere they reached the door, the paper fluttered out of her hand, and Guenever sank crouching above it, sobbing.

"Prayer—penance—this from thee, Launcelot? Thou wilt avenge Arthur; and then—for thee also a cloister and sin's atonement? Ah, Launcelot, Launcelot!"

They heard naught but her voice sobbing his name as they went down the corridor. It echoed still in their ears after they had mounted and ridden forth rapidly on their way to Camelot.

CHAPTER TWENTY-FIVE

The • Lady • of • Anguish •

The Castle of Camelot, ruinous and deserted, lay gray in the distance, and the sunset sky was red beyond. Grass grew tall and wild on lawn and terrace, and owls hooted dismally in the shaking towers. The rose-bower was a ruined and trampled wreck, Mordred's hordes having passed over it on their way to battle. Yet around the stone bench upon which Dieudonnée had sat when Anguish first told her of his love, the roses had escaped the general ruin. Around it still twined the creeping vines; and one bush, fair and perfect, yet bloomed beside it, bearing roses of pure white. The chapel bells chimed not, although it was the hour for Angelus. They hung in the castle, silent and deserted like all else.

To the rose-bower at that time Anguish came with faltering steps, and eyes expecting at once disappointment and fulfillment. At the castle gates, the monk had left him bidding him go to the rose-bower, and await his lady there. So amid the ruins. Anguish sought the rose-bower, finding it a ruin also; half dreading that his high hopes would fall also; yet with infinite faith in the monk who had been his leal comrade through many weary days.

He entered and seated himself on the stone bench; sat there and waited, his eyes fixed upon the ruined castle, his heart beating with remembrance and hope. It was the hour of Vespers; but no bells now sounded their invitation to benediction. In the rose-bower Anguish presently knelt him down and with pure heart said his Pater Noster and Ave Maria. Rising, he began a vesper hymn of Whitsuntide—"O, gloriosa Domina!" He paused. "Dieudonnée!" he whispered. Even as he spoke, a rustle of leaves made him turn; and Dieudonnée parted the low screening branches.

Lightly as a bird coming back to her nest, she came over the long grasses that had so trammeled his footsteps. Without surprise he saw at last what he had so passionately desired to see; and she took the place that was hers. As he held her in a long embrace, while spirit spoke to spirit, the gray scarf about her head fell back, and disclosed her golden hair in soft, short curls.

"When and why?" he asked, touching them gently.

"So long since I have forgotten when. And why? For love of thee."

He kissed her, although he did not understand.

"Look," she went on, lifting her face to his; "listen! Seest thou not in mine eyes those into which thou hast looked no long time since? Hearest thou not in my voice tones which thou hast known many months?"

He looked at her searchingly, gravely, again haunted by an elusive memory. She laughed, and put her hand up to her short golden curls.

"They were black a little while ago," she said. "How careful I have been to keep them covered since I began to let them grow golden again, that thou mightst not know too soon."

Still he looked puzzled; and she smiled up at him with a hint of her old mockery.

"Anguish, Anguish, whom didst thou leave there at the castle doors?"

"Brother Trestriste," he answered, not yet understanding.

"Be not grieved," she said, smiling at him. "Brother Trestriste is no more. I left what made him in a little room back there in the castle, whose secret door none knew save Queen Guenever and myself. There I put on these garments which had been there since Dieudonnée became—ah, Anguish, at last! To be so near these years and yet thou didst know me not! I cannot tell whether it was most pleasure or most pain. Hold me closer. Ah, yes! Now I know thou wilt never let me go."

"Not even to death," he murmured.

"Ah, no, not then," she answered clearly. "Death cannot part us in our love's eternity."

They stood in silence for a moment. Ruin was about them, death and desolation a recent memory, a near and possible future. Still the roses bloomed, and in the cloudless sky the moon was rising.

"Let me sit here," she went on, loosening her arms from about his neck, "here on this stone bench where first thou didst tell me—many flowers are dead and withered, Anguish; but here are white roses still; white roses for a bridal—for a burial— who knows? It matters not. We have found love."

She looked up at him, her hands lightly clasped, her great eyes sombre, yet at peace.

"I should have told thee at first," she said; "but it was so beautiful to be loved. I had never been loved before. I wronged thee by my silence. But now I may tell thee—"

He stayed her with a gesture.

"It needs not between thee and me—" he said. "I do not seek to know. It is enough that I have found thee again, and that I may take thee to my heart. Thou art Dieudonnée, God-given, whom God to me has given at last."

She looked up at him, and the old shadow came again into her eyes. Then a smile drove it away forever. He knelt beside her and kissed her hand.

"It has been worth the pains," she breathed.

A moment later, both rose.

"Let us go," she said. "Life is before us, perchance; if not, eternity."

He looked up at the calm stars.

"I must again to Launcelot in France," he said, "and do there what devoirs may befall me. The land is unsettled, dear; the times are wild and warlike. Once more we go forth together, ignorant of what may come; only I know thee now for what thou art, perfect wife, perfect love."

"As thou hast made me, dear my lord," she answered.

They stood an instant longer, side by side. Then they went away together. A nightingale began to sing suddenly in the silence.

er us go, she said . Life is before us . .

Several questions remain unanswered at the conclusion of the story. What did Dieudonnée tell Anguish on the eve of their wedding? What is the identity of the Black Knight, and why did Hellayne tell Anguish to ask Dieudonnée in order to find out? In editing this work, we came up with the following hypotheses:

Q: What did Dieudonnée tell Anguish?

A: Based on a later conversation Anguish has with Brother Trestriste, Dieudonnée may have committed the same "sin" that Anguish had with Hellayne: she was not a virgin when she married Anguish. This explains her distrust of priests, who would have considered this an unredeemable sin. Since Dieudonnée later says she has never been loved before, we may surmise that her previous relationship was not a loving one—much like Anguish's relationship with Hellayne, which is characterized by coercion and lack of consent.

Q: Who was the Black Knight?

A: The mysterious Black Knight who attacks Anguish in the forest may be Dieudonnée's former lover/husband, which is why Hellayne tells Anguish to ask Dieudonnée about his identity. In this case, he would also be the ghostly menacing face

Dieudonnée sees hovering over herself and Anguish in Merlin's vision.

ABOUT THE AUTHOR

Sara Hawks Sterling was born March 4th, 1874 in Philadelphia Pennsylvania to Dr. John Sterling and Mary Eldridge. She spent her life in the Philadelphia area working as an English teacher at various educational facilities. She authored several books in her lifetime and was considered an authority on Shakespeare. Largely forgotten today, she was an early female contributor to the Arthurian and Robin Hood canons.

She died December 26th, 1936 of pneumonia, which she caught after directing a Christmas play for the Philadelphia High School for Girls.

ABOUT THE ILLUSTRATOR

Clara Elsene Peck, born April 18, 1883, was an American illustrator, painter and commercial artist. Her works appeared in the Metropolitan Museum of Art traveling exhibition in 1956 and 1957. She was a member of the National Association of Women Painters and Sculptors, National Association of Women Artists, the New York Watercolor society, and she was one of the first 20 women to be admitted to the Society of Illustrators.

Peck did illustrations for Cosmopolitan, Good Housekeeping, The Century Magazine, Proctor and Gamble, MetLife and others. Early in her career she did several book illustrations, which remain some of her best known work today.

www.ingramcontent.com/pod-product-compliance
Lightning Source LLC
Chambersburg PA
CBHW070934250626
47159CB00009B/3249